THE
DAUGHTERS *of*
VICTORY STREET

BOOKS BY PAM HOWES

The Bryant Sisters

1. *The Girls of Victory Street*
2. *Wedding Bells on Victory Street*
3. *The Mothers of Victory Street*
4. *The Daughters of Victory Street*

The Lark Lane Trilogy

1. *The Factory Girls of Lark Lane*
2. *The Shop Girls of Lark Lane*
3. *The Nurses of Lark Lane*
4. *The Midwives of Lark Lane*

The Mersey Trilogy

1. *The Lost Daughter of Liverpool*
2. *The Forgotten Family of Liverpool*
3. *The Liverpool Girls*

Rock 'n' Roll Romance Series

Three Steps to Heaven

'Til I Kissed You

Always on My Mind

Not Fade Away

That'll be the Day

Fast Movin' Train

Hungry Eyes

It's Only Words

THE
DAUGHTERS *of*
VICTORY STREET

PAM HOWES

bookouture

Published by Bookouture in 2022

An imprint of Storyfire Ltd.
Carmelite House
50 Victoria Embankment
London EC4Y 0DZ

www.bookouture.com

ISBN: 978-1-80019-749-7
eBook ISBN: 978-1-80019-748-0

Dedicated to the memory of Don Everly, February 1937–August 2021, and his brother Phil, January 1939–January 2014. The fabulous Everly Brothers duo, now reunited in Rock'n'Roll Heaven, sharing your amazing harmonies with the angels. Thanks for all the wonderful musical memories you leave us with. Xxx

ONE

Mary Rogers made her way towards her home on Prince Alfred Road, feeling sick to her stomach. She'd just been enjoying her fortnightly shampoo and set at Madame Hettie's on nearby Picton Road when a news bulletin had come on the wireless that had shocked everyone in the salon to the core. Hettie always had the BBC *Light Programme* playing in the background, so her clients could relax to the music requests on 'Housewife's Choice' followed by a repeat of the previous day's 'Mrs Dale's Diary', while they enjoyed a bit of pampering. The newsreader's announcement that His Majesty, King George VI, had died peacefully in his sleep at Sandringham House had stunned the women into silence. Not much stopped them gossiping, but now the discussion about why the daughter of Mrs White from the nearby butcher's shop had called off her engagement stopped abruptly. The official news from Sandringham had been given at ten forty-five, and the newsreader went on to say, 'The king retired in his usual health, but passed away in his sleep and was found dead in bed at seven thirty this morning by a servant. He was fifty-six years of age and was known to have been suffering from a worsening lung condition.'

The collective gasp from Hettie's clientele was followed by a shocked silence as the newsreader's solemn voice continued. 'Princess Elizabeth, who is at the royal hunting lodge in Kenya, immediately becomes queen at the age of twenty-five. She has been informed of her father's death, and is preparing to return to London, but a thunderstorm has delayed the departure of her plane. She is expected back tomorrow afternoon, when she will take the Royal Oath, which will seal her accession to the throne.'

Hettie shook her head, tears already beginning to leave a trail down her brightly rouged cheeks. 'Well, I don't know what to say,' she began, as she took the curlers out of Mary's blonde hair and ran her fingers through the length. 'We've all known he's not been a very well man for some time now, but what a blooming shock. Oh, and that poor girl of his, not long married and the two little ones to see to, and then having to take on all them duties as the next queen of England. She's hardly had any time at all to enjoy her young family.'

Mary sighed. 'Such terrible news. And like you say, poor Princess Elizabeth. Hopefully, Philip will prove to be a godsend to her, and they've got nannies to help take care of the children. But it's not the same as looking after them yourself, is it? She'll miss out on so much of them growing up. I believe she's only gone to Kenya out of duty, because the king was too poorly to go on the visit himself. She was just standing in for him.'

'Bless her, it will have been such a shock to get told that awful news when she's so far from home,' Hettie said, smoothing Mary's fringe down and then giving the ends of her wavy hair a gentle flick out. 'Let's hope the weather improves over there and they can get that plane home tomorrow. Her mother will need her; she must be in such a state, the poor woman.' She placed her hands on Mary's shoulders. 'Now then,

I'll just bring a mirror over and you can check if the back is how you like it.' Hettie walked across the salon and picked up a large hand-held mirror in a wooden frame.

'You okay, Dolly?' she asked a lady who was wiping her eyes on an embroidered hanky as she sat under the dryer. Dolly nodded and blew her nose loudly.

'Think that sad news has got us all feeling like we could do with a good cry,' Hettie said, standing behind Mary and holding the mirror up at the back of her head so that she could see the reflection of her hair in the wall mirror in front of her. 'How's that, love?'

'It's really nice, thank you,' Mary said, turning her head from side to side, and gently patting her waves.

'Would you like a spray of lacquer? It's a bit breezy out there. It'll keep everything in place while you walk home.'

'Please,' Mary replied. 'And I've got a silk scarf in my coat pocket, so I'll pop that on my head to help protect it.'

Mary left the salon and hurried across Picton Road. She cut across The Mystery Park that ran parallel to Prince Alfred Road, and let herself into the grand Georgian townhouse that had been her family's home since just before the war ended. She wiped her feet on the doormat and dashed down the hallway to the large back sitting and dining room, where her pale-faced friend Fenella Jenkins was seated on the sofa under the window, clutching a mug in her shaking hands. A coal fire burned brightly in the grate of the marble fireplace and the wireless played quietly in the background. Fenella had inherited the large house following the death of her pilot husband, whose family home it had been. Fenella had kindly invited Mary and her girls to live with her after a bombing raid on Victory Street had damaged their house.

'Mary, oh, Mary,' Fenella began, tears running down her cheeks. 'Have you heard the terrible news?'

Mary nodded, taking the half-full mug from Fenella's hands

before she dropped it on the fawn-coloured carpet. She placed it on the nearby coffee table, took off her coat and headscarf, flinging them both over the back of a dining chair, and sat down beside Fenella on the sofa.

'Hettie had the wireless on in the salon,' Mary said. 'I can't believe it. I'll go and make us a fresh pot of tea. I need one, with extra sugar, desperately.' She dashed into the kitchen, filled the kettle and placed it on the gas hob to boil. She leant against the sink and sighed. Thankfully, the house was quiet. Usually at this time of the day there was only her and her oldest daughter Bella, and Bella's daughter Elizabeth, at home, as everyone else was at either work or school. She always savoured the peace and quiet as the front door closed on the last one to leave in the mornings. But she was glad that Fenella was not at work today.

Mary poured two mugs of strong tea and sugared them well. She carried the mugs through to the dining room, placed them on the coffee table, and sat back down on the sofa. 'Is our Bella still out?' she asked. 'I know she said she was walking to school with Levi and then popping round to Edie's for a brew and a catch-up.' Bella was married to Fenella's only son, Bobby Harrison, and the two women shared a granddaughter, three-year-old Elizabeth, known as Lizzie. They also shared a ten-year-old grandson, Levi, Bella's son, whom Bobby had adopted as his own. Bella's much adored and talented mixed-race boy was the result of a brief affair with a married American pilot during the middle years of the war.

'Yes she is,' Fenella replied. 'Didn't she say they were going into the city for shopping and then all meeting up with Bobby for a spot of lunch?'

'Ah yes, now you mention it, I think she did. I don't know whether I'm coming or going, the news has put me in a bit of a daze.' Mary took a sip of tea as a loud knock on the front door sounded. She frowned. 'Who the devil can that be? We're not expecting anyone, are we?'

Fenella half-smiled. 'Not that I'm aware of. But there's only one way to find out. Your hair looks lovely, by the way, Mary. Beautifully waved. Hettie does a good job. Martin won't be able to take his eyes off you,' she teased.

Mary blushed slightly as she hurried to answer the impatient knocking. She hoped Martin, their driver and general maintenance help around the house and the city premises they ran the entertainments agency from, *would* like it. They'd been doing a spot of courting for the last few years, nothing too serious, and he was taking her to the pictures tonight. 'I'm coming,' she shouted, trying to keep her mind on the more sober matter of the day's sad news. 'Hold your flipping horses.' She flung open the door, about to berate whoever it was for forgetting their key, and gasped as she saw her old friend Ethel Hardy standing sobbing on the doorstep. 'Oh, my goodness, Et, come on in, chuck. You've heard the news, I take it?' She stepped back to let Ethel inside.

'What news?' Ethel asked, choking on another sob and wiping her eyes with a damp hanky.

'On the wireless, earlier,' Mary said, frowning. 'The king's died this morning. Isn't that why you're crying?'

Ethel shook her head and her hand flew to her mouth. 'Oh, no. I've not heard any news today. How awful!'

'Come on through,' Mary invited, leading the way to the dining room, where Fenella nodded her greeting and gestured to the sofa for Ethel to join her. 'Sit down next to Fen,' Mary said, 'and I'll pour you a mug of tea. I've a fresh pot brewed, and then you can tell me what's wrong.' Mary hurried into the kitchen. She added an extra spoonful of sugar to the two Ethel usually took in her tea, dashed back and handed Ethel her brew. She sat down on the sofa opposite her. 'So come on, tell me what's up. If it's not the king dying that you're so upset about, what on earth is it?'

Ethel took a sip of tea and muttered, 'Thank you for this,

Mary; it's just what I needed.' She took a deep shuddering breath and shook her head slowly. 'I'm in shock. I've had some bad news. I'm just on my way back from the doctor's. You know them tests he sent me to the Royal for the other week, for that trouble I'm having down below?' She indicated with her hand in the general area of her body. 'Well, he's only gone and got the results back. They say I've got cancer of the womb, and I've got to have it all taken away.' She took another deep breath and continued. 'A complete hysterical something or other, he called it. I should have asked him to write it down. I get all mithered with them long-winded medical words they seem to call ailments these days.'

Fenella caught Mary's eye and chewed her lip. Amused though she was by Ethel's term for her diagnosis, this wasn't the time to smile. She cleared her throat. 'I think what he probably means is that you need a complete hysterectomy, Ethel,' she said gently. 'I'm so very sorry, love. What an awful shock for you. Did the doctor give any indication of how long it will be before you have the operation?'

Ethel shook her head, tears welling again. 'He said the hospital will be writing to me with all the dates and details soon. No more than a few weeks, he said. It's a damn good job we've got that National Health Service all set up properly now. At least I don't need to worry about the cost of things. I doubt my old Lloyd George insurance policy would have covered such a big job as this.'

'Oh, Ethel,' Mary said, feeling close to tears. She gave her friend a big hug. 'I'm so sorry, chuck.' Ethel was her best pal; they'd known each other years and had worked together as cleaners both before and during the war at the nearby Olive Mount Hospital. 'I suppose the NHS is something to be thankful for,' she agreed. 'I remember a woman we worked with years ago having one of them big operations like that. She joked that she was having it all took out and a mantelpiece put in. Do you remember, Et? She was quite poorly for a while, but she did recover eventually.'

Ethel half-smiled and nodded. 'Dolly Hargreaves – I do remember her, yes. She never came back to work, though, did she?'

'Well, no, she didn't. But it made a new woman of her and she lived for a good few years after her operation, so let's look on the bright side.'

'Well, I have no choice but to go back to work as soon as they say I can,' Ethel continued with a sigh. 'I've no other income, apart from a bit of railway widow's pension from losing my husband. I can't live on peanuts. I don't know what I'm going to do.' Ethel's late husband Bernie, a handsome and kindly West Indian immigrant who had worshipped the ground she walked on and whom she'd defied her family to marry, had worked on the railways and was killed doing his job, the result of a serious accident.

Fenella leant over and patted Ethel's arm. 'Don't you worry about that right now. We'll help you out where we can. That's what friends are for. You just need to concentrate on getting yourself right.'

Mary nodded her agreement. 'You bet we will. And your boys will help as well. They've both got good jobs – I know they've got families to support, but they're good lads and will see you right. Let us know as soon as you hear anything more from the hospital. Now drink your tea and we'll listen to the dinnertime news for an update from the palace.' Mary shook her head slowly. 'What a blooming awful day. And it's not even dinnertime yet. You never know what's around the corner, do you?'

Fenella nodded. 'Perhaps it's as well we don't.'

Bella Harrison and her friend Edie Collins listened open-mouthed to the news broadcaster's solemn voice. The pair were seated in the Kardomah café on Church Street in the city centre, enjoying a coffee and a toasted teacake, with their little ones, Edie's three-year-old Dennis and Bella's little Lizzie, who were tucking into jam tarts and milk, when the music playing quietly in the background was interrupted by a news update. The manager turned up the volume on the wireless and a shocked silence descended over the crowded café as each customer stopped talking while the news of the king's death was announced. Bella clapped a hand to her mouth, her brown eyes filling with sudden tears. 'Oh no. How very sad.'

'Awful news, and poor Princess Elizabeth,' Edie said. 'I hope she manages to get home safely to her mother and her children soon.'

Bella nodded. 'What a horrible shock for her. Well, I think that puts a dampener on our shopping trip, don't you? Shall we go back home and see how our mams are doing? Mine will be so upset and so will Bobby's mum. They loved the king. They always said his positive Christmas Day speeches helped get them through the war. We'll pop into the studio first and let Bobby know we won't be meeting him for lunch. Fen's at home today, she's asked her assistant Emily to take charge of reception. Emily will get them all a bit of lunch in.'

Bella asked for the bill, paid for their elevenses and the pair tucked their little ones into the trolleys they'd parked outside the shop, still clutching pieces of sticky jam tarts, and made their way to Bold Street where the entertainments agency was located. Her mother-in-law Fenella was married to Basil Jenkins and between them they owned the agency, Bold Street Enterprises, although Fenella left running the studio side to Basil while she managed the reception area.

Emily, Fenella's young assistant, greeted them from her position behind the desk in the stylish reception area. 'Have you heard the news?' she gasped, jumping to her feet and opening the door wide to allow them to navigate the trolleys through without bumping into the smart paintwork.

Bella nodded. 'Yes. Very sad, isn't it? Is Bobby upstairs in the studio?'

'He is. He's with Earl and Basil listening to some stuff they recorded yesterday. Just go on straight up, they won't mind. They pretty much stopped what they were doing when I told them the news. Leave the little ones here; they look happy enough, stuffing their faces.'

'Don't let them out or they'll put sticky fingers all over Fen's nice new sofas,' Bella warned, pointing at the two red velvet sofas positioned in the perfect place for clients to sit and enjoy a coffee before going upstairs to their music class or audition. 'I'll see if Bobby's got a clean hanky in his pocket and give them a wipe down in a minute.'

'Okay.' Emily nodded and manoeuvred the trolleys side by side away from the door while Edie followed Bella up the wide staircase to the second-floor music studio.

Bella tapped lightly on the glass door and popped her head round. 'Can we come in?'

Her husband Bobby looked over from where he was seated in front of the large window that looked out over Bold Street. 'Of course you can. We've finished what we were doing when we heard the sad news from Emily.'

'Terrible, isn't it?' Edie said. 'I know he was quite a poorly man, but still, it's the last thing we expected to hear this morning. We were in the Kardomah having a coffee when the news came on.'

'That's why we've dashed over here,' Bella said. 'We're going to go home, Bobby. Our mams will be really upset and I'm also wondering if they'll send the kids home from school early. I need to get back for Levi just in case.'

Basil rubbed his chin and Bella looked at her stepfather-in-law, knowing he was about to make an announcement.

'I think out of respect,' he began, 'we'll close for the rest of the day and go home. Bobby, you'll need to ring the mothers of your two pupils who are due piano lessons later and rebook them.'

Bobby nodded and looked at Earl. 'I'll ask Emily to do it when we go downstairs. I don't have the phone numbers up here. You okay with us closing, Earl?'

Earl smiled. 'I am. I feel we should as a mark of respect to our king.'

Bella looked across at Earl and smiled. Levi's father had emigrated from America with his daughter Dianna and sister Ruby to start a new life following his divorce. He also wanted to be a part of his son Levi's life and she and Bobby had no objections to that. After Earl had fallen in love with Bella's younger sister Molly, they had married and were now the parents of a six-month-old son, Harry, named after Bella's late father.

'Tell you what,' Earl said. 'I'll meet Levi from school and take him back to our place for a few hours. Give you guys a bit of relaxation time and he can keep young Harry entertained. I'll bring him home early evening, if that's okay.'

Bella nodded. 'Thanks, Earl. He'll enjoy that. Can Edie and I have a lift with you and Bobby then, Basil? Save us struggling on the tram with the kids and trolleys.'

'You can indeed,' Basil replied. 'We'll meet you all downstairs; I'll go in the lift with Bobby. I get too much out of breath on the stairs nowadays.'

'Okay. We'll see you down there,' Bella said as Edie and Earl followed her down the stairs. The lift was too small to accommodate more than two people. Bobby was disabled after losing half his right leg during the war and Basil struggled with his breathing from time to time. Their need for the lift was greater.

Both children smiled as their mothers reappeared. 'I've given their sticky hands and faces a wipe over with the towel out of the cloakroom,' Emily announced.

'Oh thanks, Emily. Basil would go mad if they got jam all over his nice car,' Bella said. 'I'll take the towel home to wash and Fen can bring a clean one down when she comes in tomorrow, *if* you are opening. We'll see what Basil says about that. I think the country will be in mourning for a good few days and I bet quite a lot of places will close out of respect.'

TWO

Mary ran a hand over the lilac and white candlewick bedspread and nodded with satisfaction as she looked around the spacious front bedroom overlooking The Mystery Park. The room used to be Molly's, but it had been going spare since her younger daughter married Earl and moved out of the house. Since then, Mary had always made the effort to keep the room nice and clean, and it seemed to always smell faintly of lavender polish.

Mary opened the window to let in some fresh air and as she did she peeped through the sparkling white nets at the road below and smiled as Basil's Bentley pulled up. He had been to the hospital to collect her friend Ethel, who had been persuaded by Mary and Fenella that she should stay with them while she recovered from her hysterectomy operation. Mary knew that Ethel wouldn't rest if she went back to her own home, and by staying here she would make sure that she was well looked after. It would do them both good to have a bit of company, as Mary was often on her own for most of the day if Bella was out at the studios working with Bobby. She occasionally had little Lizzie for company but it wasn't the same as having another adult to talk to. Mary was looking forward to getting her old pal on the road to recovery. She dashed down the stairs and opened the door, a big welcoming smile on her face, as Basil helped Ethel out of the car.

'Come on, queen,' Mary greeted her. 'Let's get you settled on the sofa and I'll make us a nice cuppa.'

Ethel grinned. She still looked pale, Mary thought, but once she'd got some good food inside her she'd soon get some colour back in her cheeks.

'Thanks, Mary.' Ethel took her arm as Basil followed them inside with a small suitcase.

'Leave that case at the bottom of the stairs, Basil, and I'll take it up to Ethel's room later,' Mary said. 'Are you having a brew with us?'

'No thanks, Mary,' Basil replied. 'I need to get back to the studio. I'll see you both later when I pop back to pick up Levi and Dianna. Take care, Et, it's good to have you staying with us.'

'It's good of you to have me,' Ethel said with a wide smile. 'I really appreciate it.'

Basil left and Mary helped Ethel out of her coat and took her into the dining room. 'Have a seat and I'll brew up. Do you fancy a freshly baked scone with some of my home-made jam?'

Ethel nodded. 'Oh go on then, if you insist. I can't wait to have a decent cuppa and some good food. The tea in hospital was like gnat's pee and the meals left a lot to be desired as well.'

Mary laughed. 'We'll soon build you up and have you fighting fit again.'

Dianna Franklin strolled arm in arm with her best friend Sally across The Mystery Park on their way home from school. Dianna looked over her shoulder at her half-brother Levi, who was messing around on the swings with his friend Kenny Falmer. 'Hurry up, Levi,' Dianna called. 'We're already late to meet Uncle Basil. Say goodbye to Kenny now and you'll see him tomorrow.'

'Aw, Di, do we have to go to the studios tonight?' Levi replied. 'I don't want to sing. I want to play out with my mates instead.'

Dianna rolled her eyes. 'Yes, we do. We've got to practise for that talent show Dad and Uncle Basil want us to enter. And Dad said he'd treat us to chips in a bag with a saveloy sausage for tea. You know how much you love them.' Dianna smiled as her brother's face lit up. Always the way to his heart, the promise of chips and saveloys. 'That did the trick,' she muttered to Sally as Levi said goodbye to Kenny and ran to catch up with them.

Sally sighed. 'Wish I could sing. Me mam says I sound like a cat with its tail stuck in the mangle when I try.' She laughed. 'Ah well, we can't all be good at everything, can we?'

Dianna shook her head and her glossy dark ringlets bounced up and down on her shoulders. 'You're clever, much cleverer than I am. I want to do well at school but I find it so hard at times to concentrate. It's very different here to how I was taught in America. I felt like I should be back in first grade again when I arrived. I can't seem to catch up and I need to if I'm going to be a nurse like my Aunt Ruby is. I need five GCE O levels.'

Dianna had come to England with her father Earl and his sister Ruby four years ago, so the family could be closer to Levi. Since then, she had been determined to try to fit in with the other girls in her class. Being the only Black girl in the school wasn't easy, but she had quickly made friends with Sally, who was the most popular girl in their class and who always had Dianna's back if anyone dared speak out of turn to her. She was working hard to keep up with her classmates, but it wasn't always easy when stupid boys mocked her American accent if she was asked to read anything out loud during English lessons, when pupils were encouraged to read their essays. To complicate things further and have idiots teasing her about her crazy mixed-up family, her dad had married Levi's mother's sister Molly, and Dianna now had another little half-brother, Harry. But at least they all got on well and not every family can say that.

Her Aunt Ruby was a theatre sister at Liverpool Royal Hospital. Dianna longed to follow in her aunt's footsteps, but her musical father had other plans for his children. He wanted them to be big stars on the stage and was convinced he could make it happen for them. With his background as a singer in a wartime band, he knew talent when he heard it. Dianna silently disagreed. They would have to see what the future held. But in the meantime her stepmother Molly, who was her ex-teacher from school, was helping her with extra tuition to try to give her an advantage before she took her final GCE exams next year. Molly had already made enquiries and discovered that if Dianna didn't get good enough grades the hospital ran a scheme whereby you could take a separate entrance exam and begin working as a cadet nurse at sixteen before entering full training at the age of eighteen. Whichever way she had to do it, Dianna was determined that she would get there somehow.

Saying goodbye to Sally, she grabbed Levi by the hand and together they ran up the front steps of Levi's home. He banged on the front door and greeted Granny Mary with a big grin.

'Hello, my loves,' Mary said and welcomed them inside. 'Run upstairs and get your face washed and your hair brushed,' she instructed Levi, who dashed off to do as he was told. 'And put a clean shirt on as well,' she called after him. She shook her head in Dianna's direction. 'How is it that *he* comes out of school so grubby and with half his dinner down his clothes and you look like you've just stepped out of a fashion show?' she said, giving Dianna a hug.

'Because he's a boy and they're all like that,' Dianna said

with a laugh. She loved Levi's Granny Mary, who had taken Dianna under her wing and told her to call her Grandma too if she liked. Dianna *did* like having her as a grandma, as she missed her own Grammy and Grandpa Franklin from back home very much, and sometimes wondered if she would ever see them again. She looked forward to regular letters and photographs from them with all the news her grammy crammed into each letter. Her dad had promised he would take her back to New Orleans one day for a visit, but she wouldn't hold her breath.

'Uncle Basil is in the dining room waiting for you both,' Mary said. 'But before he rushes you away, go into the kitchen and you'll find a drink of orange juice and a plate of biscuits. Can't have you singing without a bit of something to give you energy, now can we? No chocolate though, as it coats the throat, and that's not good for singing, so I'm told!' Mary smiled as Dianna dashed down the hallway and Levi hurtled down the stairs. 'Here, let me sort your shirt out. You've buttoned it up all wrong.' She rolled her eyes and proceeded to tidy him up. His big brown eyes twinkled at her and she suppressed a grin and ran her fingers through his unruly black curls. He was such a beautiful child. Sometimes people would stare at them as they walked down the street, or occasionally point out to Mary that her grandson was mixed race, as if it had never occurred to her. However, she never let it bother her. From the minute she'd held him as a newborn, Mary had fallen head over heels in love with her grandson. 'Go on and get your juice and biscuits with Dianna in the kitchen,' she said as he ran off to join his sister. Mary went into the dining room, where Basil was chatting with Ethel, who now had a bit of colour in her cheeks. 'You're looking brighter already, Et,' Mary said.

'I feel it,' Ethel said. 'Just being here with you and not stuck on that ward of miserable bloody women has bucked me up no end. I feel almost human again.'

Mary laughed. 'I suppose some of them might be in pain and that makes them feel a bit down and grumpy.'

'I suppose so.' Ethel nodded. 'One of the nurses I got a bit pally with who knows my two lads said she prefers to work on the men's wards as they were more cheerful and chatty. Can't say as I blame her from what I could see.'

'My nurses were lovely when I was in a few years back after that fire at the studios,' Basil said. 'They spoiled us something rotten when Sister was out of sight. Lovely girls.' Basil had been badly affected by smoke inhalation following an arson attack at the Bold Street studios and had spent several weeks in hospital while his breathing recovered.

'I love that you've got a television I'll be able to watch as well,' Ethel said. 'What a treat. Wish I could afford to buy one.'

'You can rent them now. We rent ours,' Basil said. 'I got it from Epstein's so we could all watch the king's funeral back in February. It was quite a spectacle to see.'

'When they decide on a date for the coronation you'll have to come and watch it here, Et, if you're not fixed up with one of your own by then,' Mary invited. 'Well, you can come and watch it anyway, as we'll throw a little party to celebrate.'

Ethel smiled and nodded. 'I'd like that.'

'I think there will be a huge cause for celebration when it happens,' Basil said. 'We'll start getting ready to put a big show on. Maybe on the park with a street party like we did after the war ended and for the royal wedding. Get everyone together for a good old knees-up.'

'You do know that Dianna's not really keen on singing any more, don't you?' Mary said to Basil. 'She's got her heart set on nursing. I do wish Earl would listen to her instead of trying to put them both on stage. I doubt Levi minds as he loves to show off and sing and dance, he was born to be a performer. Dianna has confided in our Molly, who told me she's not too happy about her father's plans.'

Basil nodded. 'I know, but it's early days and she's got a while to go before she can start nursing. She *does* have a lovely voice and it seems a waste of her talent not to use it. I can't imagine that any young girl wouldn't choose a bit of travel and glamour over long shifts on a hospital ward!'

'Hmm,' Mary said. 'When the Bryant Sisters were touring they worked harder than anyone else I knew. Just don't push her too much if it makes her unhappy. She's a lovely caring girl and would make a wonderful nurse.' She stopped as the door opened and Levi hurtled into the room followed by Dianna. She shook her head. 'Just look at your face and you've only just washed it as well,' she directed at Levi. 'You're such a mucky pup, lad.' She pulled him towards her, took a hanky from up her sleeve, spat on it and proceeded to wipe Levi's sticky face.

'Yuck, Granny,' he said, wriggling away from her tight grip. 'That's horrible.'

'Yes, well, at least you're fit to be seen in public now. The pair of you go and put your coats back on and wait in the hall. Uncle Basil's ready to go now.'

Basil grinned and got to his feet. 'I used to hate my mother doing that to me,' he said.

'My lads always squirmed away from me whenever I tried to give them a cat lick,' Ethel said. 'That's made me laugh. Bless him, though. He's so lovely.'

'Oh he is,' Mary agreed proudly. 'Very lovely, but he just gets a bit grubby at times, like all little lads do.'

Earl clapped enthusiastically as his children performed their usual routine of a couple of Shirley Temple songs, plus a song that had been written for them by Bobby and himself. The *Carroll Levis Discovery Show* that he had entered the children into was due to begin auditions at the Empire Theatre next month and they had been accepted to perform their song and dance routine. Eventually the show would be moving to television, showcasing the talents of young people who were picked, with the catchphrase, 'Truly, the discoveries of today are the stars of tomorrow'. Earl hoped the kids would impress the judges as much as they impressed their family and the audiences they'd performed for in the past. 'Take a break for a few minutes,' he told them. 'Bella has brought glasses of orange juice up for you.'

Bella smiled and pointed at the tray on the desk. 'Help yourselves. There's coffee for the daddies and Uncle Basil. I'll just pop downstairs and have a word with Fenella. How's Aunty Et, by the way?' she asked Basil.

'She's doing okay,' Basil replied. 'She's settled on the sofa and looking better by the minute, thanks to your mother. She'll flourish under her care.'

'Oh, I'm so glad she's all right,' Bella said. 'Mam's been really worried about her. It was such a serious diagnosis and it's a big operation to recover from. I'm glad I was able to get a temporary nursery place for Lizzie so that Mam can look after Ethel.'

Bobby smiled. 'Lizzie seems to love going to nursery. I think we should let her go there permanently a couple of days a week if you're down here working with us. Gives your mam time to do things for herself.'

Bella nodded. 'I think you're right, we should. It's good for her to have other little ones to play with as well. Edie said she might try and get a place for Dennis, as that'll give us more time to rehearse. The Bryant Sisters need some new songs. We've got quite a few local social club bookings coming up this year, and some even as far afield as Manchester and Blackpool. I do wish Fran would come back to Liverpool. Bobby, can we have a drive over to Southport soon to see her?' Fran was their good friend and the third member of the Bryant Sisters. She had left

Liverpool a few years ago to stay with family members in Southport.

'I don't see why not. I'll ask Martin to take us over at the weekend if you like. You give her a call tonight and arrange a time she thinks will be best.'

After getting Lizzie and Levi bathed and settled in bed, Bella sat down on the stairs and took a deep breath, cradling the phone in her hands, before dialling Fran's aunt's phone number. She always felt a bit worried about talking to Fran these days as her old friend was often on the defensive. And while Bella could understand why, she felt it was now time to put the past behind them and take a step into the future. She knew that Fran still blamed herself for the studio fire that had put both Basil and Bobby in hospital a few years ago, and the racist attack by three thugs on Earl the same night, which had left him with life-threatening head injuries. But none of it was Fran's fault. She'd had no idea of Frankie's plans that night. They weren't even living under the same roof at the time. Her ex-husband and his two docker workmates were the ones responsible and they were now serving long prison sentences in Walton Gaol for arson and attempted murder. Frankie always blamed Fran for his downfall after she left him, but it was his controlling and bullying ways that had lost him his wife and baby daughter. He'd been such a loving husband at first, but then his jealousy of her friends and popularity, making a mockery of her when she wanted to work in the job she loved so much, singing with the Bryant Sisters alongside Bella and Edie, and finally his violent assaults on her, had become more than Fran could cope with. The three girls had entertained the troops right throughout the war years and still enjoyed singing professionally from time to time. But they missed Fran now she had gone with her daughter to live with her aunt and uncle for a while. They needed a change of scene while they let the dust settle and to escape the inevitable gossip. That while had turned into almost four years, and though she was sure that there was lots to love about being by the sea, Bella knew that Fran's heart would always be in Liverpool, and she felt it was time for her friend to return to her roots.

Her hand shaking slightly, she dialled the number and waited for someone to answer. 'Southport 9512,' a male voice answered. Fran's Uncle Joe.

'Can I speak to Fran, please?' Bella asked.

'She's out at the moment, love. Can I get her to give you a call when she comes home?'

'If you wouldn't mind. It's Bella calling from Liverpool.'

'Okay. Well, she won't be long. We're expecting her back within the hour. I'll pass the message on.'

'Thank you.' Bella hung up and sat quietly for a few minutes, wondering where Fran had gone. She didn't have any friends to go out with in Southport as she kept herself to herself, and it was a bit late to be out shopping with Lorraine, her little daughter, who was probably tucked up in bed at this time anyway.

Fran swung her handbag over her shoulder, picked up the carrier bag with her sweaty keep-fit clothes in and said goodbye to the other women in her class. She always refused the offer of going for a quick drink after class, conceding that she would go for coffee another day. As yet, that day had not come. Fran guessed that the women were only trying to include her, but people were naturally curious and always asked her questions about herself and why she was divorced. It was the same at the school gates when she dropped Lorraine off in the mornings. She hated discussing her personal life with strangers. She'd even changed her surname back to her maiden name after she'd left Frankie so that any new people she met wouldn't link her name with his, after his crimes were plastered all over the newspapers following the trial. Fran had no wish to be associated with him in any way and had even had her daughter's name changed too.

As she walked slowly down the road, away from the church hall, she couldn't help thinking that no matter how far away she ever ran, Frankie was somehow still controlling her life, even though he was away for many years. After a long wait she'd been granted a divorce that Frankie had been advised by his solicitor not to contest. She'd thought of returning to Liverpool to be close to her family and friends. Her mam had begged her to come home as they were all missing her, and when her brother brought her mam across to see her each month it was so hard to say goodbye when they went home. Her aunt and uncle had been very good to her and made brilliant substitute grandparents for Lorraine. But it wasn't the same. Southport was lovely, not unlike New Brighton with its long pier, floral gardens, funfair and the sandy beach that she enjoyed long walks on at the weekend with her daughter, who liked to play on the sands while Fran sat in a deckchair and read a book if the weather was nice, but it was a lonely existence. She also missed singing. A couple of times Uncle Joe had asked her to sing for events at the Royal Birkdale Golf Club, of which he was a member. She'd enjoyed herself and an accompanying pianist had asked if she'd like to work the social clubs with him at the weekends. Although flattered to be asked, Fran had refused. Singing without Bella and Edie by her side just didn't feel right; after all the years they'd worked as a trio, singing solo didn't appeal to her at all. Before she'd left Liverpool she'd started to write songs and Bobby had put the melodies to them. The songs had been recorded by other artists and Fran had been pleasantly surprised to receive royalty payments each year, which had given her a nice little income, but she couldn't rely on that forever. Now Lorraine was at school she should really be getting a job before her savings ran out.

Fran had a folder of words written for new songs. She wrote them in the privacy of her bedroom at night while the rest of the household slept, and kept the file stored under her mattress. But without Bobby Harrison's input with the melodies they remained just that: a pile of words. It really was time to have a good think about her future. She couldn't let what Frankie had done ruin the rest of her life or keep herself alienated from the people she loved. Although he was in prison, she was the one who felt trapped. She needed to get back to living her life.

THREE

Bella and Bobby were relaxing in their bed-sitting room at the front of the house when the phone rang out. Bella jumped up and hurried down the hall to answer it. She smiled as Fran's friendly greeting came down the line. 'Fran, it's so good to hear from you,' she replied. 'How are you doing, and Lorraine of course?'

Bella listened as Fran told her things were okay, but she was missing home a lot more as the weeks went by.

'Well listen, Bobby and I would love to come and see you if it's okay?' Bella said. 'Maybe this coming Sunday? We could go out and have a bite to eat and catch up. We'll come on our own. I thought we might go in the Scarisbrick Hotel for lunch and a nice drink. We don't have to worry about the kids then as Mam will look after ours, or Molly and Earl might volunteer. In fact, I'm sure they would.'

'Oh that would be lovely,' Fran replied. 'My aunty and uncle can have Lorraine all to themselves and spoil her rotten. Sounds like a good plan to me. Would Edie be able to come, do you think?'

'I'll ask her,' Bella said. 'Her mam would have Dennis, but she'll probably want to bring Stevie. Would you mind that?'

Fran laughed down the phone. 'Not at all. It would be so good to see the four of you again. It's been a while.'

'Okay, well we'll see you on Sunday about twelve-ish. I'll get Bobby to book us a table at the hotel for one o'clock. Really looking forward to seeing you again. Give our love to Lorraine.'

'I will, and you give mine to everyone back there. See you in a few days.'

Bella hung up, a big smile on her face. That had been easy and there'd been no awkwardness either. She went back to Bobby. 'All sorted. Can you book us a table for five at the Scarisbrick for Sunday lunchtime at one? I haven't asked Edie yet but I'll call her now, there's no way she'll want to miss out.'

Edie was very enthusiastic when Bella spoke to her. 'Of course we'll come. And Fran's missing Liverpool, you say?'

'She is. We need to work on her and give her the confidence to come home.'

'We do. And now's the right time, because you will never believe this, but I've just been in next door for half an hour. Rita wanted to tell me something important.'

'Oh, what's that?' Bella asked. Rita and Charlie Jepson were Edie's very good neighbours who lived in between her and Stevie, and Earl and Molly.

'Well, they'd just come off the phone after getting a letter this morning from their daughter Connie in America. She wants them to go and live over there so they can see their grandchildren growing up. I know they really miss Connie and regret turning their backs on her when she got into trouble, but they've put all that behind them and have decided there's nothing to lose and nothing to keep them here. So they are going to sort things out and apply to emigrate.'

'Oh my goodness!' Bella exclaimed. 'That *is* a turn-up for the books. They've missed so much time with the family and they're not getting any younger. They need to make the journey while they are still fit enough to cope with it.'

'That's what Rita said. They're hoping to sail on the *Queen Mary* as she doesn't fancy flying. What a lovely experience for them. They've gone into Earl and Molly's now to talk to him and Ruby about what to expect. But you know what this means, don't you?'

Bella shrugged. 'No. Tell me.'

Edie smiled. 'Well, when and if the Jepsons go to America...'

'Ah yes,' Bella said as realisation dawned. 'Of course. The house will be up for grabs. Just in time for Fran and Lorraine coming home.'

'Yep.' Edie nodded. 'We will definitely be working on her on Sunday, Bella, and as soon as she agrees I'll ask Rita to tell the landlord that there's an interested party. He knows Fran anyway as she was his tenant when she lived across the street. It's all just perfect. Fran and Lorraine will be back on Victory Street where they belong.'

'Fingers crossed,' Bella said. She said goodbye and went to tell Bobby the news. Then she hurried into the back room, where her mam and Martin were watching television with Ethel. Basil had taken Fenella out for a meal this evening. Her mam looked up with a smile.

'Are you all right, chuck? You look a bit flushed and bright-eyed.'

Bella smiled. 'I'm fine thanks, Mam. I've got some really lovely news to tell you all.' She sat down next to Ethel and spilled out her story. Her mam clapped her hand to her mouth.

'Well, that's good news all round,' Mary said. 'I'll miss Rita of course, but they need to be with the family at their time of life. What an adventure for them, though, to sail on that lovely ship. I'll pop over and see her tomorrow. And that house will be just the job for Fran and the little one. Rita and Charlie have got it lovely. I bet they'll leave all the furniture and carpets as well. They'll not be taking them in bags on the ship now, will they?' Mary laughed at her own joke. 'It's funny how things have a knack of falling into place at the right time. All you have to do now is persuade Fran to get back home. She can always stop with her mam or even here until the Jepsons have gone. We've still got a room spare in the attic.'

'Let's wait and see, Mam,' Bella said. 'I don't want her to feel pressured. She can make the decision by herself after we let her know the options.'

Fran stared open-mouthed as an excited Bella and Edie took it in turns to tell her the news from back home. Martin had dropped the four of them off outside the hotel and told them he was going to see an old pal in Skelmersdale for a few hours while they had a catch-up with Fran. He was coming back for them at five o'clock. They'd enjoyed roast dinners and, stuffed to the gills, were now enjoying a drink. 'Flipping heck,' Fran gasped. 'If that isn't meant to be, I don't know what is.'

Bella nodded. 'We said that. I know there's a while to go before the Jepsons get things in writing, but they are already making plans and have filled all the emigration forms in. Rita told Mam they've also applied for passports. So they are definitely serious about it all. As long as the authorities agree, they should be okay. Earl has told them that having a daughter and two grandchildren in the USA will help. The youngest was born there. Connie's husband has a good job with the American air force, training pilots, and their house comes with the job, so he can vouch that they will be financially supported once they arrive. And Rita and Charlie have savings of their own to fall back on. There's a self-contained annexe to the family's house that they will live in. It looks very promising.'

'I hope it all goes well for them,' Fran said. She chewed her lip anxiously. 'Do you lot think it will be okay for me to come home? Fingers won't be pointing in the street or anything?'

'Fran,' Edie began. 'You didn't do anything wrong. I'm sure it will be fine. And we'll all be there for you. You'll be tucked in between us and Earl. What could be safer? You can bang on the wall either side if you're worried about anything.'

Fran took a deep breath. 'Oh, sod it. I can't keep hiding away forever. I want my life back. Tell Rita to ask the landlord to give me first refusal on the house if they go. I'll make some plans when I get back to my aunt's. I'll talk to our Don and see if he'll come and pick us up next weekend. I can go and stay at Mam's for a while until it's all sorted. It will give me a chance to get Lorraine settled in the new school then. Phew. I can't believe it. I've made a decision. And I'm in total shock. But it's a nice feeling.'

Bella lifted her glass in a toast. 'Here's to a safe return home for Fran, and hopefully a reunion of the Bryant Sisters in the not-too-distant future.' She smiled as everyone cheered and clinked their glasses.

'Talking about the Bryant Sisters,' Fran said, bending to pick up her handbag from beside her chair. She pulled out a sheaf of folded paper and handed it to Bobby. 'I've written some more songs that need melodies. Do you want to take them with you and see what you think?'

Bobby smiled and nodded. 'Absolutely I do. We only said the other day that we need some more songs for you ladies. Leave it with me, Fran. I'll make a start tomorrow and give you a call in the next day or two. If you plan on getting Don to bring you home soon then all being well, we can start to rehearse next month.'

∾

On the drive home, Bobby sat in the front passenger seat where he had more room for his disabled leg to stretch out and Stevie was sitting in between Bella and Edie on the back seat. Martin was unusually quiet and Bella asked him if he was okay. He nodded, keeping his eyes on the road ahead, and cleared his throat. 'I've summat to ask you,' he began. 'I was just thinking,' he continued, his cheeks colouring slightly. 'My mate that I've been to see while you were with Fran; well he's just got married. First time wed for him, and all that. His new wife is a bit older than him, but they seem very well suited. She was widowed in the war like your mams were, Bella and Bobby. And well, I'm not very good at this sort of thing, but I wondered how would *you* feel, Bella, if I asked your mam to marry me? We've sort of been going around together for a long time now and everybody else seems to be taking the plunge, including Basil and Fenella. I don't want to leave it too late. I've a nice bungalow, as you all know. We could make it a proper cosy little home and I can assure you I will look after Mary very well, you need have no worries on that score.'

Bobby caught Bella's eye and smiled. She nodded her consent. 'Martin, we thought you'd never get around to it. We'd be delighted and I know I speak for our Molly here too. And Mam will be over the moon.'

'Do you really think so?' Martin said, his face lighting up in a big smile. 'What if she says no?'

'She won't,' Bella assured him. 'Just do it.'

'When would be the best time?'

'I don't think there's ever a best time,' Bobby said. 'Remember when I proposed to you, Bella, and you ran away from me because you were worried about me rejecting you because of Levi?'

Bella nodded. 'We got it right the second time, though. Just go with your gut feeling and your heart, Martin. Maybe do it tonight when we get home.'

'But I haven't got a ring,' Martin protested. 'I can't ask her without a ring and I don't even know what size she takes.'

'She's the same ring size as me,' Bella said. 'We used to share a dress ring years ago and it fitted our wedding ring fingers. Wait until tomorrow night then to ask her. I'll come with you to the jeweller's tomorrow afternoon when I come down to the studios. You can choose something and see if it fits me.'

Martin nodded. 'That sounds like a good idea. Thanks, Bella. It's good to have a woman's perspective on this and nobody knows your mam better than you do. And make sure you're all at the house after tea tomorrow night, but don't let on why. Ask Molly and Earl to be there – you'll have to drop a hint to Molly so she doesn't think I'm going behind her back in asking you and not her for permission to marry her mother.'

'You leave our Molly to me,' Bella said. 'I'll pop round and see her in the morning before I come down to the studio.'

FOUR

'At long last!' Molly exclaimed. 'I thought he'd never get round to it.' Bella had just told her sister about Martin wanting to marry their mam. 'Well, this calls for a nice coffee to celebrate and a piece of Ruby's gorgeous ginger cake.'

Bella laughed. 'Shall I call the little ones in out of the yard for milk and biscuits and go and knock on for Edie? Dennis is out the back playing with Lizzie so I'll fetch him in as well. Edie knows about Martin and Mam by the way, because she was in the car with us last night.'

'Good idea. Just clear the table of Dianna's school books and put them all on the sideboard for now. I've been giving her extra tuition towards her exams.'

'Bless her. She's such a lovely girl,' Bella said as she opened the back door and called to the children, who were playing a skipping game, organised by bossy Lizzie by the looks of things. Her blonde plaits bouncing up and down on her shoulder, one hand on her hip, she was wagging her finger at Dennis and shrieking and making gestures with her hands as though she was telling the little boy off for not turning the rope that was attached to the washing line post properly. Little Harry, who was the exact image of Levi at the same age, was sitting in his trolley by the back door, clapping his hands and laughing. Blond-haired, blue-eyed Dennis – the spit of his mother Edie – looked a bit fed up, Bella thought. However, the mention of milk and biscuits had him beaming from ear to ear and running indoors to Molly while Bella tapped on Edie's open back door. 'Coffee and cake time at Molly's!' she called.

'Oh goody, I'm on my way,' Edie called back. 'Just dashing up to the lavvy first.'

Bella grinned and made her way back into Molly's modern fitted kitchen. Having upstairs bathrooms was such a treat compared to how they all used to have to hurry up the yard to the old row of brick-built toilets that was now used as a store for bikes and gardening stuff. Bella shuddered as she recalled the many spiders, the odd mouse and how the cold weather used to cause the cisterns to freeze. Thank goodness for progress, although she was aware that many families in Liverpool still got by with outside facilities with no hot running water or baths. Bella would never forget her humble beginnings – the tin bath in front of the fire on a Friday night shared by the whole family – and would be forever grateful for what she had now.

With the little ones seated at the dining table, tucking into their snack, Molly led the way into her immaculate front room and placed a tray of coffee and Ruby's ginger cake on the coffee table. 'It's more tidy and peaceful in here,' she said. 'Help your-selves; sugar is in the bowl as I never know who takes what these days.'

'This cake is yummy,' Edie said, rolling her eyes. 'So moist and spicy. Ruby is such a good cook.'

'She certainly is,' Bella said. 'Levi is always telling us about his Aunty Ruby's yummy cakes.'

'We usually have this warm with ice cream,' Molly said. 'It's bloody delicious. So, ladies, are we going to do a little surprise party for Mam and Martin tonight then?'

'That's a good idea,' Bella said. 'Me and Edie are in the studio later though so we haven't really got the time to make anything. Martin is getting the ring this afternoon when I'm with him. He's definitely giving it to Mam tonight. I'll have a quick word with Fen, see if we can grab a few ready-made sausage rolls and stuff. Can you make a nice Victoria sponge, Molly?'

Molly nodded. 'Yes, I've got baking things in so that's no problem. I'll ice it and put "Congratulations" on the top. I'll make sandwiches as well and then we'll bring them over after tea; if I bring them over sooner Mam will smell a rat. Just try and keep her occupied, you know how nosy she is.'

'We'll ask Basil to get some drinks on his way back from the studio,' Bella said. 'One way or another we'll have a nice little party and she'll love the surprise.'

'Let's hope so,' Molly said, raising her eyebrows. 'So what else did you get up to in Southport then, apart from agreeing to marry our mam off?'

Bella smiled and told Molly about Fran wanting to come home soon.

'Ah right, well, she'll be needing somewhere to live.' Molly jerked her thumb at the wall towards the adjoining house. 'Next door's moving soon,' she said. 'The Jepsons, that is. Well, they hope to be. Off to America to live with their Connie and her family.'

Edie nodded. 'We know. We're keeping our fingers crossed that the landlord will agree to Fran having the house.'

Molly let out a sigh of relief. 'Phew, that's good. He'll probably give her first dibs on it as he knows her and knows she'll pay her rent on time. I was hoping someone decent would get it. You never know, do you? There's some scruffy devils about that let the street down. Be good to have another nice neighbour, and the little one can play with our boys when she's not in school. If she's anything like your Lizzie she'll soon have them organised.'

Bella laughed. 'Lorraine is just like her mother and probably twice as bossy, so I'm sure she will. Harry and Dennis had better watch out.'

'Be nice to have a little girl nearby,' Molly said, and then smiling secretly she continued. 'I wasn't going to say anything yet... Please keep this to yourselves – I think we may have another little Franklin on the way. I'm going to see the doctor on Friday for the results of the sample I took last week. Keep your fingers crossed for us. Earl won't say anything until we know for sure, we haven't even told Ruby or Dianna yet, although I think Ruby half suspects as she heard me throwing up the other morning and asked if I was okay. Fortunately I haven't felt or been half as sick as I was with Harry in the first few weeks so maybe it's a change of sex that's responsible for that. This time we're hoping it might be a girl. I know it's a bit too soon after having Harry really but these things happen, don't they?'

'Oh, Molly, they sure do.' Bella threw her arms around her sister. 'You're going to have your hands full. But that's wonderful news. I'll keep everything crossed for you. Can I tell Bobby though please, and we'll keep it from Mam to surprise her?'

'Of course you can. But tell him not to say anything to Earl just yet. Otherwise Fen and Emily will get wind and that will be it, and then Mam will go mad because she'll be the last to know.'

'We'll keep, err, *mum*,' Edie teased, laughing. 'I'm so happy for you, Molly. Stevie says it's time we got cracking again, but I like working and if Fran comes home we're hoping to be busy again doing shows. So we'll have to see. I suppose we'd better make tracks, Bella. I need to take his little lordship round to my mam's place and then come back and get changed out of my cleaning gear, ready for the studios. I'll be round at yours just before one, then we can get the ten-past tram down to the city.'

'And I'll get on with baking the cake and making sand-wiches for tonight,' Molly said. 'See you at yours about seven, shall we?'

'Yep.' Bella nodded and got to her feet. 'Bring Ruby if she's not on shift and Dianna as well. I'll go and grab Miss Lizzie from the back room and I'll see you both later.'

Bella rolled her eyes at Bobby behind her mother's back. Mary had just popped into their room, announced that she was going to have an early night, and if no one wanted the bathroom she was going up for a nice long soak. Bella quickly took charge of the situation and told her mam to follow her into her and Bobby's downstairs shower room, where she kept her toiletries. It would be great if her mam was in the bath and out of the way for the next half-hour or so while they retrieved the hidden food from the cellar, where it was in the spare fridge that was as a rule only used at Christmas. She checked her watch. Molly and family and everyone else would be arriving soon and she wanted to get the table laid.

'Mam, here you are.' She handed over a bottle of lavender bath oil. 'This smells lovely. It'll help you to relax. Go on; make the most of a bit of peace. But don't go to bed just yet. Come back down and we'll all watch a bit of telly and have a nice drink. Ethel will enjoy that. She loves the company after being on her own at home.' She hoped she sounded convincing enough and prayed that her mam wouldn't come down in her old dressing gown and slippers with a turban over her hair. Fingers crossed anyway. She breathed a sigh of relief as Mary took the bottle of bath oil and went upstairs. She heard the lock slide into place on the bathroom door.

. . .

The noise of running water drowned out the knock on the front door and Bella let in her sister, Earl, and their family. She placed a finger on her lips as she ushered them all down the hallway to the back rooms.

'Where is she?' Molly whispered, looking over her shoulder.

'Getting in the bath with my posh bath oil,' Bella said with a grin. 'I'm just keeping my fingers crossed that she doesn't come downstairs afterwards in her holey slippers and manky dressing gown. You know what she's like: not that keen on surprises unless it's her doing them. Right, let's get everything on the table. Martin's in our room with Bobby. He's nervous as hell, bless him, but the ring is safely stashed away in his pocket and should fit perfectly. I won't tell you what it's like as that will spoil the surprise for you, but I'm sure Mam will love it. Basil, will you sort the drinks trolley out and get the glasses lined up for a toast please.'

'Leave it with me,' Basil replied. 'Everything's in order.'

Fenella was just coming up from the cellar with her hands full as Bella, Molly and Ruby hurried into the kitchen and unloaded the bags of food Molly had brought.

'Can you get the rest of the stuff from the spare fridge, Bella dear,' Fenella said. She spotted Molly unwrapping her beautiful iced cake and placing it on a white lace doily on a silver stand in the middle of the table. 'That looks absolutely beautiful, Molly. Well done. Oh this is so exciting. I love a secret party. Mary will be so thrilled.'

'Well, let's hope so,' Bella said and told Fenella of her concerns regarding what her mother might choose to wear after her bath.

'Don't you worry,' Fenella said. 'As soon as I hear her pull the plug I'll go upstairs and tell her we've got some unexpected visitors from the studio who would love to meet her. I'll make sure she puts on a nice dress and brushes her hair well. Leave it with me. Now let's get everything onto the dining table ready.'

'So who *are* these people?' Mary asked a hint of suspicion in her voice. 'I didn't hear anyone come in. And why the devil do they want to meet *me* anyway?'

Fenella smiled and airily waved her hand. 'Just a few nice musicians, who really enjoyed your scones last week when you sent a tin in for the workers,' she gabbled, plucking the lie from somewhere. 'They were, err, just passing and thought they'd call on spec to see if we were in. Anyway, it's best to make a good first impression, don't you think?' She lifted a blue cotton floral-print dress with a sweetheart neckline and front button fastening from Mary's wardrobe. 'This one always looks so nice on you and the blue really brings out your eyes.'

Mary stared at her and pursed her lips. 'Fenella Jenkins, you're up to something! You've gone all shifty-eyed. Nobody ever just calls here on spec. What's going on?'

Fenella laughed. 'Nothing. Don't be so suspicious. And see, you've bobby-pinned your hair up so the steam from the bath will have helped to set it beautifully. You know how it always waves so nicely, Mary. Right, I'm just popping into our room for something and it will give you time to get dressed and take your pins out. See you in five minutes.'

She hurried out of the room and Mary shook her head after her. There was no peace in this blooming house. All she wanted to do was get into bed and read her new Agatha Christie library book. She'd been looking forward to starting it all afternoon. There'd be murder on Prince Alfred Road at this rate if she didn't get some time to herself, never mind *The Murder at the Vicarage*. She sighed and began to take out her bobby pins, running her fingers through the curls they'd left behind. She rummaged in her drawer for fresh underwear and then slipped her blue dress over her head and fastened up the mother-of-pearl buttons on the bodice. Fen was right; it *did* echo the blue of her eyes nicely. None of her daughters looked like her; they all favoured her late husband Harry with their dark hair and big brown eyes. Even her youngest, Betty, who she'd lost to diphtheria when she was just five years old, had been the spit of her daddy. Mary smiled. The only one remotely like her was young Lizzie, but Bobby was also blond and blue-eyed. Still, it was the best and closest she was ever going to get to anyone favouring her. Fenella knocking at the door again disturbed her reverie and she called, 'Come in.'

'Oh, you look lovely, Mary. Have you some nice lipstick to wear?'

Mary sighed and picked up her Max Factor Truly Pink. She pursed her lips to slick them with colour. Then, smacking them together, she smiled and dabbed a touch of lippy on each cheek, rubbing the pink in to give her a bit of a glow. 'There, will I do?' she said.

'You certainly will,' Fenella said. 'You look lovely. Right, let's go downstairs and meet our guests.'

Out on the landing Mary frowned and said, 'It sounds very quiet down there. I can't hear a soul talking. Are you sure we've got visitors?'

'*SURPRISE!*'

Mary nearly jumped out of her skin as the door to the dining room was flung open by Fenella and everyone shouted at once. Her jaw dropped as she realised all her extended family was there as well as Edie, her hubby, and little lad. 'What are you lot doing here? What the heck's going on?' she gasped. 'It's not me birthday 'til next month.' She glanced around and pursed her lips. 'And where's the unexpected visitors you told me about, Fen?'

Ethel, who was seated on the sofa under the window, burst out laughing. 'She fell for it then?'

'Fell for what? What you on about, Et? Will somebody please tell me what's going on?' Mary repeated. She stared at Bella, who whispered something to Martin, and he stepped forward, his face flushing slightly.

'Err, perhaps I should explain,' he began. 'Now, strictly speaking this little party isn't down to me; blame your daughters for that. But I'd like to ask you something, Mary.' He turned to Bella and she nodded encouragingly, mouthing, 'Go on.'

Mary's hand flew to her mouth as Martin got down on one knee and held out a small red leather box. 'I think you know how I feel about you, don't you?' he said as she slowly nodded, her eyes never leaving his. 'Well, if you feel the same, would you do me the honour of becoming my wife, Mary?' He opened the small box to reveal a pretty gold ring with a solitaire diamond surrounded by tiny rubies, nestled on a bed of black velvet.

Mary felt her eyes filling with tears as she nodded and then cried, 'Of course I'll marry you, Martin, yes, of course I will.' She helped him to his feet as everyone cheered and clapped and he took her in his arms and dropped a kiss on her lips before placing the ring on her finger.

'Oh, thank God for that,' he gasped as the family crowded around and hugged, kissed and congratulated the couple and admired Mary's beautiful ring.

'This calls for a toast,' Basil said, pouring champagne into assorted glasses and handing them round. He poured lemonade for the little ones and said, 'Now, raise your glasses to Mary and Martin, a match made in heaven if ever there was one. We all wish you a long and happy life together.'

'To Mam and Martin,' Bella and Molly said at the same time. Bella smiled through her tears. 'I'm so happy for you both.

Thank God you said yes, Mam, after us lot telling him to just get on with it.'

Mary laughed and hugged her girls in turn. 'Thank you, my loves. I'll never forget your dad, you know that, don't you. But I know Martin will look after me and I'm very lucky to get another chance at happiness at my age, and in this uncertain world we live in.'

From her seat on the sofa and holding her glass high, Ethel smiled. 'You're a lucky bugger, queen. But this couldn't happen to a better person. Congratulations to the pair of you.'

Mary laughed. 'Might be your turn next, Et.'

'I doubt it,' Ethel said. 'I'm just happy to be alive and enjoying being part of your lovely family for a while.'

Standing by the dining table with a big smile on her face, Fenella clapped her hands to gain attention. 'Congratulations to the pair of you. I think we should start the buffet before Levi and Dennis fade away from starvation. They've not taken their eyes off the sausage rolls since they walked into the room.'

'Why not,' Mary said, laughing. 'Go on, lads, get stuck in.'

FIVE

With a big smile on her face, Molly left the doctor's surgery and hurried home to a peaceful house. Dianna was at school, Ruby on an early shift, and Mrs Jepson next door was looking after Harry for an hour while Molly had attended her appointment. She let herself in and picked up the phone in the hall, sat down on the stairs and dialled the Bold Street studio number, butterflies doing somersaults in her stomach as she pictured Earl dashing to the phone. But it was answered by Emily.

'Hi Emily, it's Molly. Is Earl available to talk please?'

'He's upstairs in the studio, Molly,' Emily replied. 'I'll give him a shout. One moment please.'

Molly heard Emily hollering up the stairs and then Earl's deep voice answering as he shouted for her to transfer the call through. Molly smiled as he spoke, a hint of excitement in his voice.

'Moll, how did it go, my love?'

'It went very well, Daddy,' she replied, grinning as he gasped.

'Oh wow! Really? That's wonderful news. Are you okay

about it? I know it's a lot sooner than we planned to have another.'

Molly laughed. 'I'm fine. It's not due until early November. We'll manage and Harry will be walking and hopefully almost out of nappies by the time it arrives, with a bit of luck.'

Earl laughed. 'We'll work on him. Can I tell the guys now?'

'You can. I'm going to get Harry and then dash round to tell Mam and catch Bella before she leaves to come down there to you lot. I'm so excited, Earl. I know we thought there was a good chance of it being a yes, but it's still nice to have it officially confirmed, isn't it?'

'My darling Molly, it's the best news. Can't wait to let them know back home.'

'Talking of home, there's an airmail letter here for you and Ruby and on the back of the envelope it says it's from your brother Scotty. It arrived as I was leaving for the doctor's.'

'Oh, that's great. I haven't heard from him for a while. Wonder what he's been up to lately? Be good to catch up with him. See you later, darlin'. Wait until I come home before you tell Ruby and Di. Let's do it together after our evening meal.'

'We will, see you later, love you.'

'Love you too.'

The front door to the Prince Alfred Road house stood wide open as Molly pushed Harry's trolley up the ramp at the side of the front steps that had been built for Bobby's wheelchair. Not that he used it any more, but the ramp was handy for prams and trolleys. 'It's only us,' she called, rattling the letter box. 'Why is the door wide open?' she asked her mam, who had appeared in the hallway, a puzzled expression on her face.

'I didn't know it *was* open. Come on in, love. Bella,' she called over her shoulder, 'did you leave the front door open?'

Bella came out of her and Bobby's sitting room into the hall, looking as bemused as their mam was. 'No. I closed it when we came in. Oh, oh, where's Lizzie?' She looked around worriedly. 'I thought she was in the kitchen with you, Mam.'

'And I thought she was in there with you,' Mary replied. She dashed into the dining room at the back to Ethel. 'Has our Lizzie been in here with you, Et?'

Ethel looked up from reading her *Woman's Weekly* magazine. She shook her head. 'No, love. I haven't seen her since she went out with Bella to take Levi to school earlier.'

'Oh my God, she must have got out,' Bella exclaimed. She hurried to the door and looked up and down the road. Across on the park she spotted a flash of the red dress Lizzie was wearing today and blonde plaits bobbing up and down, as the little girl ran across the grass towards where several fairground hands were setting up rides and stalls in readiness for next week's Easter holidays fair. 'There she is. Lizzie, Lizzie!' she called. 'Stop right there.' Bella dashed across the road to catch up with her adventurous daughter, who ignored her frantic cries, excitedly pointing at the fair. She stamped her feet when Bella caught hold of her hand and pulled her back towards the park gates. 'Okay, madam. We're going home right now and there'll be no more treats for you this week. You're a very naughty girl,' Bella scolded. 'Wait until I tell Daddy what you've been up to.'

Lizzie seemed totally unimpressed by the threat and burst into tears. 'Go see horses,' she screamed, kicking out at Bella's shins and pointing to several tethered ponies. Bella slapped her legs and dragged her screaming off the park and up the steps to the front door where her mam and Molly were watching the scene unfold.

'Can you believe that?' Bella exclaimed, pushing Lizzie inside and slamming the door shut. 'I didn't even know she could unlock the front door. God, anything could have happened then. There are some dodgy-looking blokes putting the rides together. They might be harmless, but you just don't know who you can trust, do you?'

'No, you don't, 'Mam agreed. 'You're a very naughty girl, frightening your mammy like that, Lizzie. No biscuits for you today.' She shook her head as her granddaughter simply stared at her.

'She can go and sit in her room for an hour to teach her a lesson,' Bella said, marching her daughter into the hall and pushing her towards the stairs. 'Off you go and stay up there until I say you can come down again.' She shook her head as Lizzie stood still and ignored her. Bella dragged her up the stairs and pushed her into the bedroom. 'Now stay there,' she ordered, wagging her finger at Lizzie, who shrugged her shoulders and sat down on her bed. 'Levi was a little angel at her age,' Bella muttered, making her way back downstairs. 'I don't know where she gets it from.'

'Boys do tend to be a bit quieter until they grow up,' Mam said. 'That one was born a little madam. Takes not a blind bit of notice of anything you tell her. She doesn't get it from our side!' She pursed her lips. 'It'll be from Fenella's family. She was a wilful one when younger, for all her airs and graces now. Right, let's have a brew,' she finished as Bella caught Molly's eye and raised an amused eyebrow. Any bad behaviour was never down to Mam's side of the family, she was always quick to point out.

Bella and Molly took Harry into the dining room to see Ethel, who insisted he stay with her while mother and daughters had a catch-up in peace in the kitchen.

'So what brings you round here, chuck?' Mary said to Molly as she poured mugs of tea. 'Thought you usually went shopping on a Friday morning?'

'Not today, Mam,' Molly replied. 'I had an early appointment at the doctor's.'

Mary frowned. 'Why, what's up? You're not poorly are you, love?'

Molly smiled and looked at Bella, who winked. 'No, Mam. But I have got some news for you. I'm, err, I'm expecting another baby. The doctor just confirmed it.'

Mary's jaw dropped. 'Oh, love, that's a bit quick off the mark after Harry, isn't it? Still, never mind, it can't be helped. But how will you manage? Harry's only a baby. Not even walking yet. It'll be hard work for you.' Mary shook her head. 'Ah well, what's done is done – congratulations, lovey.'

Molly laughed. 'Thanks, Mam, I know it's quick, but I'll cope just fine. It's not due next week, you know. I've got a good few months yet. I've got Ruby and Dianna to help me as well as Earl. There are plenty of hands on deck. Think we might need a bigger house. Earl wants to buy something of our own with a nice garden anyway. He's been saving like mad for a deposit. We'll have to start looking sooner rather than later now, though.'

Bella smiled. 'Well congratulations, sis. Let's hope if it's a girl it's better behaved than madam up there.' She jerked her thumb towards the ceiling and laughed. 'She's a one.'

Earl took the lead later that night as the family gathered around the television set to finish watching Dianna's favourite comedy show, *I Love Lucy*. She'd told him it reminded her of home, although life at Grammy and Grandpa's place was never quite as chaotic as the Ricardos' TV household. It was just nice to hear familiar accents besides her dad's and Aunt Ruby's.

'As soon as this show finishes,' Earl began, 'Molly and I have something to tell you. In fact, we have two wonderful announcements to make.' He'd got home from work before Ruby and had read his brother Scotty's letter. He'd give it to Ruby to read the finer details later, but for now he wanted to see her face light up when he told her just what Scotty was intending to do. As the closing credits appeared on screen and the theme tune finished, Earl jumped to his feet to switch off the set. He stood in front of the tiled fireplace and smiled secretly at Molly, who got up to stand beside him. 'Okay,' he began. 'To start with, we have a new family member on their way and they will be arriving sometime in November.'

Dianna frowned. 'A new family member? Who exactly is that and where are they coming from?'

Earl laughed and patted Molly's slightly rounded stomach. 'From right in there, but we don't know who they are just yet, until they arrive. Might be another little brother for you, or maybe even a sister for a change.'

Ruby laughed and got to her feet. 'Well, that *is* good news. Congratulations to you both.' She gave her brother and Molly hugs, her face alight with joy.

'Dianna?' Earl said. 'Are you not going to say anything, honey?'

Dianna stared at him and shook her head. 'I hope you're kidding me, Dad?'

Earl frowned. 'No, honey. Why would I be kidding you? We're expecting a new baby. I thought you would be happy and pleased for us. Our little family is growing.'

Dianna rolled her eyes. 'Where will we put it? We have no room in this house as it is. And people at school will make fun of me even more now.' She burst into tears. 'How could you, Dad? Do you ever think about anyone other than yourself?' She jumped to her feet and headed for the door, but Earl pulled her back into his arms.

'Hey, hey, what's all this about? Of course I think about you all the time; you're my little girl! But why do you think people will tease you more? What's that all about? It's got nothing to do with anyone else. This is *our* family and we do what suits us best.'

Dianna grimaced and pulled away. 'You just don't get it do you? Being the only Black girl is hard enough around here. But you producing more kids is so embarrassing, especially at your age.'

Molly bit her lip and tried not to look amused. Earl glanced at her and shrugged his shoulders. 'We're not quite elderly and past it yet, Dianna,' he said. 'And as for where they will sleep, well I am going to buy us a house very soon. And listen, honey, I know it's not always easy for you being different, but you hold your head up high and don't let anyone make you believe that you're not perfect just the way you are.' He smiled. 'Oh, and as for being the only Black girl around these parts, that's going to change fairly soon too, if all goes according to plan.'

'What do you mean?' Dianna glared at him, her big brown eyes loaded with suspicion.

'What I mean is, in the not-too-distant future your Uncle Scotty, Aunt Dolores and your cousins Tammy and Ebony are coming to join us in Liverpool.'

He was heartened to hear Ruby's surprised gasp and thrilled to see a slow smile spreading across Dianna's face. Scotty was Earl and Ruby's youngest brother. Earl's son Levi was named after Levi and Scott, two of the Franklin boys. Earl felt the weight lift from his shoulders as he gave his daughter a hug. Having been the victim of racist insults himself, he knew it wasn't always easy for her, but she'd get there and with her twin cousins, who were almost the same age as Dianna, in tow, she would be able to walk in that school playground for her last few months with her head held high. He handed Scotty's letter to Ruby. 'It's all in there, sis, they're making their plans right now.'

SIX

Fran gazed out of the grimy window of her brother Don's work van as they rattled down the Picton Road towards her old family home. All her stuff was packed and loaded into the back. Lorraine was squashed in between her and Don on the front bench seat. She'd fallen asleep with her head on Fran's lap, her thumb plugged firmly into her mouth. It had been hard saying goodbye to her Aunty Rose and Uncle Joe after being with them for such a long time, but she'd promised to bring Lorraine back to spend a week with them in the school summer holidays, if she wasn't too busy working. Since she'd given him the lyrics to the new songs she'd written, Bobby had done as promised and put melodies to most of them. Over the phone he'd told her that everyone at the studio agreed they were great and she couldn't wait to hear them and hopefully sing a couple with Bella and Edie very soon. Three weeks had passed since their visit and her making the decision to come back to Liverpool. She'd had to wait an extra couple of weeks longer than she'd first planned, as Don had been working non-stop it seemed, and the van wasn't free for him to borrow until today. But at least it had given her that extra bit of time to mull things over in her mind and to make absolutely certain that she wasn't rushing into things and making a mistake.

Her mam had been overjoyed when she found out that Fran and Lorraine were coming home. They had spoken on the phone several times since and she knew her dad was excited too. They had offered to do as much child-minding as Fran needed while she got her career back on track. Her elderly granny, who had lived with them all Fran's life, had sadly passed away last year and now they no longer had to look after her, they both had more time to spend with their granddaughter. Fran had returned home briefly for the funeral but had then come straight back to Southport on the train. Her old bedroom had been redecorated and was ready and waiting, and her dad had picked up a small camp bed for Lorraine to sleep on as there was no room for another bed in there. She still had her furniture in storage from when she left Liverpool and if she got the Jepsons' house eventually then at least she had a head start. She would buy a few new bits and pieces as and when she could afford them, including a nice bed for her daughter. Edie had told her that so far the move to America was all going to plan. She'd also said that Earl's brother and family were in the middle of their own plans to come to Liverpool. It was all change for everyone right now, but hopefully things would fall into place in time. She just hoped that no one would tell Frankie about her moving back home. Some of his cronies lived in the area and were no doubt still in touch with him, by letter or even visits to the prison. She knew from Frankie's sister that his family had completely washed their hands of him, so his old so-called friends would be all the outside support he had. She felt a bit nervous thinking that he may still be made aware of her movements even while inside, but she just had to be brave and get on with things, otherwise he would have won; and she couldn't allow him to ever control her life again. Maybe one day she would meet another man she could trust and feel safe with.

She wasn't looking for anyone right now, but she could live in hope.

On Monday morning Sally called for Dianna to walk to school. The girls linked arms as they strolled across The Mystery Park towards Wavertree Church of England School, housed in a stone building known as Rose Villas. Dianna was still feeling a bit fed up with her dad and Molly, but so far, apart from the family, no one else knew that another baby was on the way. They'd had a busy weekend, with Fran coming home to Liverpool, and everyone had been invited to tea over at Bella and Bobby's place on Sunday afternoon to welcome Fran and Lorraine back. Apart from music and getting the Bryant Sisters back up and running again, the conversation had been mainly about Uncle Scott and his family and their intended move to the UK, and how Molly and Dad had looked at a couple of houses but weren't too keen on the locations. Molly didn't want to live too far away from Granny Mary and Bella but most of the tall Georgian houses on Prince Alfred Road were too expensive for her dad to buy. They were going to see another place later this week on Queen's Drive, which wasn't too far away. Molly had told her it looked lovely on the picture she'd seen in the estate agent's window – an affordable price, semi-detached, with four bedrooms including a converted loft area. Molly had said that meant Dianna could at last have her own room instead of sharing with Aunt Ruby. She didn't really mind sharing with her aunt, though, and if Dad and Molly moved out then she could have her own bedroom if she decided not to go with them. She thought she might stay on with Aunt Ruby during the week as Victory Street was closer to school, and then stay with her dad and Molly at weekends, if her dad would allow her to. It would be much quieter at Aunt Ruby's for doing her homework. Granny Mary and Martin had booked a date for their wedding, which was to take place in July. Uncle Basil said they'd have to put on a show for the wedding buffet. If her cousins had arrived by then, they could sing together as they'd done in the gospel choir back home. Everyone used to say the Franklin girls sang like angels. Dianna had agreed that she would love to sing with Ebony and Tammy again. She was getting a bit sick of singing the childish songs her dad and Uncle Basil liked her to perform with Levi. At least with her cousins around they could sing songs more suited to young ladies. She and Levi had the *Carroll Levis Discovery Show* auditions coming up next week. They were to be held at the grand old Empire Theatre and she was dreading it. She was going to have to put on quite a show if she were to impress on the enormous stage, and truly her heart just wasn't in it.

'You okay, Di?' Sally asked, squeezing her arm. 'You're very quiet this morning.'

'Yeah,' Dianna replied, shrugging her shoulders. 'Just got a lot on my mind, I suppose.'

'Would it help you to talk about it? I'm a good listener and I can keep things to myself.'

'I know you can and I appreciate that,' Dianna said. Sally was indeed a good listener and would never repeat anything she was told in confidence. But really, what was there to say or complain about compared to what a lot of girls her age were going through? No matter what career she ended up having, she was far better off than many in her class who were from large families, and were destined for menial factory work or domestic duties. Most had no choices other than to get any job they could find as soon as they left school, to help support their families. Dianna had a nice home and good parents. Molly was a lovely stepmum and she never once felt neglected, not like she had done when she lived with her birth mom. After her parents' marriage broke down when

Dad came home from the war, that had been a terribly difficult time. Her mom had always been drunk and there was usually a different man staying in the apartment each night, asking her to call him 'uncle'. They used to give Dianna the creeps, the way they looked at her, but her mom never even seemed to notice. She was so glad that he had come to her rescue and taken her to live with him and Grammy and Grandpa Franklin. She was so glad to be out of and away from her mother's lifestyle. So what if Dad and Molly were expecting again; it didn't mean they wouldn't love her and Harry and Levi as much as they did now. She needed to learn to be a bit less uptight and ignore what other people thought or said.

'Sorry, Sal. I'm worrying about my exams before end of term. What if I fail them? And then Dad wants me to go on stage and I want to be a nurse. I just don't know what to think, say or do at times.' That would do for now, Dianna thought. No point in loading all her anxieties onto her friend's shoulders.

Sally nodded. 'You'll be fine. All the extra tuition Molly is giving you will make a difference. Try not to worry too much. Just go in the exam room on the day with a determined head on your shoulders. And I'll do the same. We will be nurses one day. And we'll be blooming good ones too.' She smiled as they entered the school playground. 'There's your brother with his mum and little Lizzie,' she said as Levi waved at them.

Dianna watched as Levi said goodbye to Bella and ran across to her. Dianna gave him a hug and she turned to smile at Lizzie, who was screeching her name and tugging on Bella's hand. Bella walked over and shook her head at Lizzie.

'She's being a nuisance again,' Levi told Dianna. 'Bet you're so glad she doesn't live at *your* house.'

Bella laughed. 'Now there's a thought. I think we'll swap her for Harry. He's such a good little boy, just like you were, Levi.'

Lizzie beamed at the suggestion. 'Want to live wiv you and Aunty Molly,' she said to Dianna, jigging from foot to foot.

'Oh you heard that then?' Bella said. 'Funny how you only hear what you want to hear, isn't it?' She shook her head.

Dianna laughed. 'I think we'd be sending you straight home after just one night.'

'And *I* think you would be too,' Bella agreed. 'Oh God, I am so looking forward to a day at the studios when I drop this one off at the nursery, a day of peace and quiet. Much as I've said I wouldn't mind another, I don't envy our Molly one bit. But then she's the mother-hen type, takes it all in her stride, as she no doubt will with this next one. She loves kids and was always a great teacher. The children she taught here all loved her. Right, I'd better get off. See you later, son,' she said to Levi. 'See you soon, Dianna.'

As Bella strode away, Sally stared at Dianna, one eyebrow raised. 'Is Molly expecting again?'

Dianna looked down at her shoes and nodded. 'I didn't tell you because I feel so embarrassed.'

Sally shook her head. 'There's no need to feel embarrassed, Di. It's what parents do. Look at our house, with six of us kids already and another on the way.' She sighed heavily. 'I dream of having a room of my own – even a cupboard or a shelf that no one else is allowed to touch would do!'

Dianna nodded. 'It's just that people will talk,' she muttered. 'I mean, Dad's got Levi with Bella and then there's me and then there will be two with Bella's sister, at least, by the time they've finished. It all seems such a muddle. I mean, what relationship is Lizzie to me? She's Levi's half-sister and so am I. Does that make Lizzie my half-sister too? It's very confusing.'

Sally frowned. 'I'm not too sure, to be honest. I don't think you're really related. Ask the biology teacher to work it out for you. She'll be able to tell you. Now come on, put a smile on that pretty face of yours and let's get inside. The sooner we start, the sooner it'll be break time. I feel exhausted with this morning already, and it's not even nine yet.'

Dianna smiled. 'How do you think I feel at times? My head is constantly in a whirl, like it's going to explode.'

~

Bella, Fran and Edie finished rehearsing one of Fran's new songs, the upbeat 'Summertime of Love', singing like they'd never been apart. They did a little dance up and down the studio floor, working out a new routine.

'Wow!' Bobby exclaimed as they finished. 'That was amazing. Just like old times. A real Bryant Sisters song if ever I heard one. Well done, Fran. You've definitely got a future as a songwriter as well as a singer.'

'Absolutely fantastic, girls,' Basil said, clapping enthusiastically, while Earl cheered. 'Right, it sounded fabulous even with just Bobby's piano accompaniment, but tomorrow I will have a band lined up. We need some brass in there and a rhythm section and that young guitarist we signed a few weeks ago; he was really good, he can sit in with you as well.'

Earl nodded his agreement. 'You've got your girls back, Basil. Back where they belong.'

Basil smiled. 'Next thing on the list is outfits. I presume you still have some of the old clothes from the war days?'

Bella nodded. 'We've all still got our military uniforms; they just need dry-cleaning to freshen them up. We can wear those when we do our Andrews Sisters spots, but we do need new dresses for our Bryant Sisters sessions. We've all gained a pound or two from having babies. I know my dresses are a bit tight in places now I'm a bit curvier.'

Edie and Fran nodded their agreements and said, 'Us too.'

'There's a new dressmaker just up the top of Bold Street,'

Bella continued. 'We should go in and have a chat with her, see what she can do for us.'

Fran smiled. 'She has some lovely dresses in the window that would be ideal for stage work. Bet she'd do us proud, and we'd be supporting a local business as well.'

'Good idea,' Basil said. 'I'll give Emily a shout and ask her to bring us up a tray of coffee. I think we deserve it. I'll send out for cakes as well – that's if you're not all on diets after talking about curves.'

As he finished speaking there was a light knock on the studio door, and Fenella popped her head around. 'Everything all right?' she enquired. 'Was that the girls singing that very lovely song just now?'

'It was,' Basil replied. 'Lyrics written by our Fran here, the melody composed by your son.'

'Well I have to say, it sounded wonderful. I wasn't sure if you'd got the wireless on. Are you going to record it?'

Basil nodded. 'We will do when the full band are in. We'll do a few recordings and try and get them out on sale for the autumn. I was just about to holler down for coffee. Can you get Emily to do the honours and ask her to nip out for cakes? And would you mind making an appointment for these three with the new dressmaker down the street, please, Fen.'

'Leave it with me,' Fenella replied.

By the time Bella arrived home late that afternoon her mam had already fed and watered Levi and Lizzie after school and nursery and the pair were outside in the back garden, supposedly helping Martin to take down an old shed that had been falling apart for ages. Rita Jepson was sitting at the kitchen table having a brew with her mam. Bella nodded a greeting and flopped down on the chair next to Rita. 'How's it going? Any news on your move to America yet?'

'It's all going smoothly as far as we can tell,' Rita replied. 'We've had the interviews and medicals and the passports have arrived. Just waiting for them to officially say yes or no now and then we can get the passage booked and give notice on the house. The landlord is in agreement that Fran should have it when we go. Would you ask her to call round when she gets a minute, love? There's no point in us chucking out decent curtains if she can make good use of them. There are a few bits of furniture she might like as well.'

'I'm sure she'll be very grateful,' Bella said. 'It's hard starting over again when you're on your own, especially with a little one to support.'

'It'll be all change round there when Earl and Molly move on as well,' Mary said, pouring a mug of tea for Bella. 'Sugar it yourself, love,' she said, pushing the glass bowl towards her. 'I can never remember who takes what these days.'

'You're as bad as Molly,' Bella said with a chuckle. 'Two for me, as it's always been, Mam. And with regards to Earl and Molly's house, he told us today that Ruby wants to stay on there in Victory Street. She says it's handier for her travelling to the Royal as she sometimes gets a lift from a lady ward clerk in the next street, and if and when Scotty and his family arrive she will have the room to put them up until they find a home of their own. She'll also have Fran and Edie for neighbours and she gets on well with other people that live nearby too. There's a lot of respect for Ruby in the area, her being a nursing sister, and I have a feeling that Dianna may want to stay with her. Earl says she's not very happy with him and Molly and the fact that there's a new baby on the way.'

'Oh dear,' Mary said. 'Bless her, she's at an awkward age and doesn't quite know what she wants from life just yet. I remember feeling that way, although God knows the world's a very different place from when I was her age. Maybe staying on her own with Ruby will help her feel more secure. Dianna has had a lot to contend with in a short time – neglect from that mother of hers, and then coming over here and trying to get settled in. Meeting Levi, then Earl marrying Molly and young Harry putting in a quick appearance, didn't really help. It was too much to take in all at once, and now this other baby on the way. I know it's been hard for her to adjust after being an only one for so long, and it doesn't help when you get gangs of stupid lads name-calling because she's Black.'

'She's beautiful and worth ten of those scruffy louts,' said Bella. 'She's such a caring girl with a lovely kind nature and would make a fabulous nurse. I just hope Earl sees that side of her before it's too late.'

Dianna took a deep breath as her dad and Uncle Basil, sitting in the audience with the parents of all those taking part, clapped and cheered when she walked on the stage with Levi at the Empire Theatre. She swallowed hard and smiled. Before she'd left the house, Molly had piled her glossy ringlets up on top of her head and fastened them in place with a big red bow that matched her full-skirted satin dress with the sweetheart neck-line. Levi looked equally smart in a matching red shirt, black trousers and waistcoat, his textured curls for once tamed into place. Bella and Bobby smiled proudly as their son took a bow when the youngsters were introduced to the audience. Carroll Levis spoke to Dianna – his soft Canadian accent was not that much unlike her own American drawl – and asked her which two songs they had chosen to sing as Levi rocked on his heels beside her. She told the host the names of the songs that had been picked for them. The show was to be recorded and would be broadcast on the BBC *Light Programme*, so at least Dianna was happy that she wouldn't be seen on a television screen singing the songs her dad and Basil had chosen for them. She wished they'd realise that she was no longer a little girl and was sick to death of doing an impersonation of Shirley Temple – albeit a Black Shirley Temple rather than a white blonde-haired one – but they still wanted her to have her hair curled in a similar fashion, with the big childish bow fastening it all up on top, when she preferred her hair down on her shoulders. All she wanted now was to get tonight over with, get her end-of-term exam results, and then if they were as good as she needed, she would tell her dad that was it, no more, she'd had enough.

She gritted her teeth as the pianist played the opening bars to 'Animal Crackers in My Soup'. When she'd asked her dad if they could maybe sing one of the new songs that Fran had written instead of such a babyish number, he'd said it was a commercial song that everyone would know. She'd heard him telling Molly how good Fran's songs were, but he'd said those songs were for the Bryant Sisters and as yet no one would know them. She half-heartedly began to sing along, with Levi throwing himself into the words and doing all the actions he'd seen Shirley Temple doing in the film. She reminded herself that this was good for him and even though she didn't want a career on stage, Levi said he did, so she summoned up some enthusiasm.

The clapping and cheers when the song ended were enough for Dianna to know they had done their best and she took a curtsey alongside her brother, who was taking a proud bow. Then the pianist played the intro to their next song and it was one that Dianna loved and she knew Levi did too. 'The Whole World in His Hands' always filled her with joy, as it reminded her of singing it in the gospel choir back home.

~

Earl felt himself bursting with pride as his children took their final bow and walked offstage to clapping and loud cheers from the audience. He turned to Basil, who nodded with satisfaction.

'Best act tonight without a doubt,' Basil said.

'I hope so,' Earl said. 'Dianna didn't look too happy at first, though, did she? But she perked up eventually.'

'Well, since you brought it up, Earl,' Basil began carefully 'I think you may need to have a father–daughter talk to her and soon. I know you're only trying to encourage her talent but if performing is not what she wants then it will only make her unhappy. Mary told me that she has her heart set on becoming a nurse. Maybe Dianna needs to try for that and see how she gets on. If it's not right she'll come back to us and we'll welcome her with open arms, but it has to be Dianna's decision and hers alone.'

Earl nodded. 'I will. There's plenty of time. She's got her exams soon and then a year to do her GCE coursework, then we'll see if she can get a hospital training place, *if* it's what she really wants. I think living with Ruby when me and Molly move will be good for her too. I'd just like her to follow in my footsteps, the chance to travel and have a better life. A chance to be special rather than different.'

'Well, hopefully your brother and his kids will arrive in a few months, which might change how she feels.' Basil looked up. An announcement was being made on stage of the winners' names. 'Here we go,' he said as the third in line's name was called out. A young girl who had tap-danced and sung came running on stage. In second place were two young boys, one with a guitar slung around his neck.

Earl held his breath as Carroll Levis called for silence while he read out the winners' names. Seated further along the row, Bella gripped Bobby by the hand.

'The sister-and-brother act of Levi and Dianna Franklin were clear winners tonight,' Carroll Levis announced, and the pair came shyly back on stage to be presented with a winners' certificate and a small trophy.

'Told you,' Basil said, a big smile splitting his face.

'You sure did. That certificate will look great framed and on the wall in our studios.' Earl beamed with pride as the audience clapped and cheered his kids once more.

Bobby sighed and Bella gave him a hug. 'They only changed Levi's surname to Franklin temporarily,' she reminded him. 'It makes sense if they are billed as a brother-and-sister act. We know he's a Harrison like us.'

'I suppose so,' Bobby said, his tone one of reluctant agreement.

SEVEN

'Oh, they've set a date at last,' Mary exclaimed as the midday newsreader on the wireless announced that the coronation of Princess Elizabeth to be crowned queen would take place a year from now, on 2 June 1953 at Westminster Abbey. 'Not before time either. They were saying in the hairdresser's the other week that Winston Churchill is responsible for the delay. All that political stuff shouldn't come into something as important as this, surely.'

Martin flicked ash into an ashtray on the coffee table. 'Politics can be the root of all evil at times. Winston got us through the war and now the opposition wants him out. He'll always get my vote, no matter what happens.'

'One thing they all should be looking at now is getting the rationing over and done with. I mean, still only being allowed two bob-worth of meat per person a week is just ridiculous. Time it was scrapped and life started to get back to normal, especially the food side of things. The war's been over six years now and we are having to shop almost as thriftily as we did back then. There are kiddies in Liverpool that still haven't tasted chocolate, even though sweet rationing was supposedly over last year. Thank God for your mate and his smallholding. At least we never go short of eggs and chicken as well as vegetables. We're a lot luckier than most families.'

'We are, Mary. Talking of my mates, I've managed to get hold of my handyman pal; he's coming along to the bungalow tomorrow to have a look at the wall in the sitting room that's got some damp in it. Once he's sorted it out I'll repaint the room and then you can choose some new floor coverings. They all need replacing as they were my mother's choice and are a bit threadbare now, as well as not very fashionable for today. I know you like the more modern look.'

Mary smiled. 'That will be lovely. I'll look forward to getting it all nice for us. I might be able to get some curtains from Paddy's Market. They always have a nice selection of second-hand good-quality curtains for peanuts and I can alter them to fit. I feel so excited when I think about having my own home again. Oh I know Fen has been good in taking us all in to live here, and telling me that it's my home too, but I've always felt a bit like a lodger, so it will be good to have the feeling of being the lady of my own place once more.'

'Lady of the manor, eh? Well, lady of the bungalow, anyway.'

Mary laughed. 'Something like that, and no more stairs to climb to save my poor knees. I can't wait.'

'Well, not too long now, my love. Four weeks and we'll be husband and wife. I can't wait either.'

Fran took Lorraine to school and then walked round to Rita Jepson's house with Edie, who had just dropped young Dennis off at the nursery. Bella had told her yesterday that Rita had asked if she'd pop round. 'Can't wait to get the keys, all being well,' she said as they knocked on the door. 'I hope they hear something soon.'

The door flew open and Rita smiled a welcome. 'Come on in, girls. Charlie's just gone to get a newspaper and his ciggies. I'll pop the kettle on while we wait for him to come back. It's good to see you again, Fran. How's that little girl of yours? Has she settled in at school?'

'She loves it thanks, Rita. She's settled really well. She also loves all the fuss she gets at Mam's from her uncles and granny and granddad. They spoil her rotten.'

'I'm sure they must have missed her,' Rita said. 'They'll be making up for lost time. I can't wait to meet my two grand-children.'

'Have you had any news yet, then?' Fran asked.

'Yes, we've had a letter first thing this morning. We've been accepted. It's such a relief. We're going into the city tomorrow morning to book our passage on the *Queen Mary*. I'm so excited. I can't quite believe it. As soon as we have a sailing date we'll give a week's notice here. That's all the landlord said we needed to give as he knows you're ready to come in as soon as we go. Have a seat while I brew up. The kettle's just started to whistle.' She hurried into the kitchen and left the girls alone.

Edie smiled at Fran as they perched on green leather-look armchairs either side of the cream-tiled fireplace. 'I bet that's a relief, Fran.'

'You've no idea how much,' Fran said. 'I can't wait to be back on Victory Street and in my own home again. It's been a long time waiting – well, counting the time I spent in South-port, I mean – but I'm nearly there now.'

Rita brought a tray of mugs through and put them on the dining table. 'Now, Mary tells me you already have some furni-ture that you stored before you went away, but if there's anything here that you fancy just let me know. We're only taking a few personal effects, some photographs and the like. Our daughter has furnished the annexe we'll be living in, so we won't need anything else and whatever you want we are happy to make a gift of it to you.'

'That's really kind of you, Rita. Thank you so much. My brother checked on my stuff in storage last week and said there had been some water leakage in the unit a few months back, so some things are damaged and will need to be chucked away. I'll be very grateful of anything you can spare, I really will,' Fran said.

'We'll have our tea then and I'll show you round,' Rita said. 'It will be a huge help to us not to have to empty the place, especially if we can get a sailing quite quickly – such a big weight off our shoulders.'

'Would you like to come with us and look round, Edie?' Rita said as the front door opened and Charlie walked in.

'No it's okay. I'll keep Charlie company while you take Fran to view,' Edie said with a smile. 'I'll go and pour him a mug of tea.'

'The cosy is on the pot in the kitchen so it should still be warm enough,' Rita said as she beckoned for Fran to follow her upstairs.

By the time Fran and Edie left the Jepsons' house, Fran was the proud owner of almost all their furniture, their good-quality carpet squares and tasteful curtains. There was a small glass-fronted china display cabinet in the front sitting room that would be going to Edie's mam's house as Fran thought it a bit too fragile to be in the same house as her daughter, who she was concerned might fall into it and break the glass. Lorraine was forever doing cartwheels and clumsy tipple-overs, even indoors. It was a nice but delicate piece of furniture that would be much safer with Edie's mam, who would love it, Rita was assured.

'I can't believe how lucky I am,' Fran said as they walked across the park to tell Bella the good news. 'She's even leaving me her pots and pans. All I need to do is hang our clothes in the wardrobes and I'm sorted. The single bed in the spare room was bought brand new for her daughter in case she ever came back home, which of course she never did. It's not even been slept in once and they did the room out so nice as well, all pink and white. Lorraine will love it in there. And the double bed is fairly new as well, Rita said. I could never have afforded all that, not for ages anyway. I want to get them a nice gift to take with them, but what? You and Bella can have a think and help me. It can't be anything big as it will need to fit in their suitcases. Three heads thinking are better than one.'

'I know what you can give them,' Bella said. At her house, she, Fran and Edie were having a good think about a suitable going-away gift for the Jepsons. 'If Basil can get a record of our songs made in time we could sign our names on it and then they'll always have a reminder of their time here. He might be able to get a sample copy produced, if not the real thing; and what about a lovely picture in a frame of the Three Graces? It will be their last glimpse of Liverpool's waterfront as they sail away. Lewis's or Blacklers might have something like that in their home department.'

Fran nodded. 'That sounds like a good idea. We'll ask Basil about the record when we're in the studio later and I'll have a look round the shops on Saturday morning for a nice picture. Nothing too big and heavy, but something they can hang on their wall in the new place that will always remind them of home.'

Mary walked into the dining room in the middle of the girls' conversation. 'So I guess they've heard and are definitely going then?' she asked.

Fran nodded. 'They've got the letter today and are booking their passage tomorrow. So it shouldn't be too long now.'

'Right.' Mary nodded. 'Well, as soon as they have a date and are packed and ready, we'll ask if they want to stay here for a day or two and we'll throw them a leaving party and then Martin can take them to the dockside and we'll all go and wave them off. I feel a bit sad in a way as I've grown very fond of Rita and Charlie. But on the other hand I'm thrilled for them that they are going to see their Connie and meet their grandchildren at last.'

The second week in July, Fran got the keys to her house and Rita and Charlie were toasted by Basil at the leaving party held for them at the Prince Alfred Road house. Surrounded by the friends they'd made since their move to Victory Street just before the end of the war, Rita felt a twinge of sadness that it was unlikely she would see any of them again. But they would write and keep in touch, and she and Charlie had so much to look forward to now, reunited with their daughter and her husband and children. It was exciting, if not a bit daunting, as she'd never left Liverpool in her life before except for the odd caravan holiday in North Wales when Connie was a little girl.

'I'm so sorry we'll miss your wedding at the end of the month,' Rita said to Mary. 'But we'll be thinking about you and raising a glass to you on that day.'

'I'll write to you and tell you all about it and we'll send you some photographs,' Mary promised.

'Did you pack the sample record we got rushed through for you?' Basil asked.

'We did, and the lovely picture of the Graces. I wrapped

them carefully in a couple of thick towels and packed clothes around them to pad them out, so they should be safe enough, and they still have the cardboard packaging around them as well. We'll always have the girls to listen to now and Connie's husband Larry will enjoy the record as well. Connie told us he saw the Bryant Sisters at Burtonwood during the war.'

'Ah, of course he did,' Earl said. 'Larry was a nice guy and I'm sure he'll be looking after your daughter and grandchildren well.'

'We're looking forward to meeting him,' Charlie said.

'We'll all be down on the dockside tomorrow to wave you off,' Basil said. 'We'll miss you both but we wish you the very best of luck in your new life.'

'And we'll certainly miss all of you,' Charlie said.

Mary blew her nose as the tugs led the magnificent *Queen Mary* from the docks and up the River Mersey to the open sea. Martin slipped his arm around her shoulders and dropped a kiss on the top of her head. She smiled up at him. 'I'm just being daft,' she whispered. 'I'm sure they'll be very happy. But I will miss them.'

'We all will,' Martin whispered back. 'But everything works out for the best in the end. Like my old mam used to say, God moves in mysterious ways. They've got what they longed ages for at last, Fran's got a lovely new home to move into and she deserves nothing less, and we've got our wedding to look forward to, as well as *our* lovely new home to move into, too. So let's wish them well and a safe journey to their new future.'

Bella smiled at her mam and squeezed her arm. 'It's going to be so quiet at our place when you move out, Mam, and Aunty Et's going back home for good tomorrow as well.'

'Oh I'll be popping in most days, don't you worry,' Mary

said. 'I'll still be seeing to Lizzie and Levi after school and nursery if you're working with Bobby. There's plenty for me to do. I'll miss our Molly just being round the corner, mind, but there's a regular tram passes the new house. So once they've moved in I can still pop round easy enough. It's all change, isn't it? Ah well, what will be and all that.'

Dianna held her breath as the results for the end-of-term exams were given out. Sally shrieked with joy as both she and Dianna learnt they'd got high enough marks to go forward for another year to do their GCE exams.

'I can't believe it,' Dianna said, her voice filled with emotion. 'This is all thanks to Molly for the extra help she gave me. Just one more year of really hard studying and we're on our way, Sal. Fingers crossed, nursing here we come!'

'It's such a relief. I know Mam could do with me working and bringing some money in,' Sally said. 'But she told me that if I did well this year she'll let me stay on. Thank goodness she's so understanding. She's always saying she wants better for me than she's had, although she seems happy enough with my dad.'

Dianna nodded. 'Well, let's enjoy the summer holidays now and have a rest. Granny Mary's wedding is on Saturday. That's the last time I will be singing with Levi if it's anything to do with me.'

'Good luck telling your dad that. He's so proud of you, and that interview he did with the *Echo* when you won the Carroll

Levis show was great. It's shut the idiots up anyway; they've not made a single nasty comment since then.'

Dianna shrugged. 'They haven't heard the broadcast yet and it's on the wireless this Friday night. I'm dreading the reaction, especially when they hear the Shirley Temple song. They'll really take the mickey then.'

'Well, *you* know that song was really for Levi. You got to sing one of your favourites afterwards.'

'We did, but even Levi is getting too old for Shirley Temple stuff. Bobby and Bella need to work on Lizzie really and get her singing, but Dad says she has a short attention span so maybe she's not cut out for show business either.'

Sally laughed as they linked arms and left the school premises. 'Who knows?'

Mary and Martin said their vows in the register office in Wavertree Town Hall on the last Saturday in July. Basil and Fenella were their witnesses and all the family and a few close friends were there to wish them well. Ethel sat with Bella and Bobby; being Mary's closest friend, she was considered to be part of the family. Martin had no immediate family but had a few friends he'd known for many years, who all attended to wish the couple well. On the steps outside the building Basil arranged everyone into groups for photographs. The reception was to be held in the church hall, where Mary's WI friends had helped with the buffet and room decorations like they'd done for Basil and Fenella's wedding a couple of years ago.

As their guests made their way to the church hall, Mary took Martin by the hand and led him to the churchyard. She had a bouquet of pink roses, the colour matching her dress and jacket perfectly, and white daisies, and she placed it on the grave of her youngest daughter, Betty, whose name was etched in gold lettering on the black marble gravestone, alongside Mary's late husband's name and his parents'. Harry wasn't buried here; his resting place was somewhere out in France with so many other fallen soldiers, but his name had been inscribed so that she had a place to come and lay flowers from time to time. Martin stood silently while Mary closed her eyes and said a little prayer. Then she turned to him and smiled. He took her hand and led her to the church hall, where their guests were waiting.

Bella re-fastened the blue ribbon bows in her daughter's hair and straightened her white ankle socks. 'Now try and keep clean and tidy for a couple of hours at least,' she warned her. 'Mammy's going to sing in a few minutes with Aunty Fran and Aunty Edie, so you stay here with Dennis and Lorraine and be a good girl, okay?' She shook her head as Lizzie ignored her and ran off across the room.

'You'll be lucky,' Bobby muttered under his breath. 'She's like a flipping whirlwind – never still.'

'I can live in hope,' Bella said with a sigh. 'I sometimes wonder if she's not quite right; does she hear me, or does she just ignore me on purpose to get attention?'

'What do you mean, not quite right?' Bobby asked, a frown appearing on his face. 'She's just being a pest as usual. It's her age. She'll be fine once she starts school. I think we were just lucky with Levi. He was always so good, except when he was with his friends and they got a bit giddy. Lizzie reminds me of the little girl Levi went to school with, the blonde one who was a handful.'

'Belinda Potter, you mean,' Bella said with a grin. 'She's actually grown up to be quite a nice girl now. Always polite when we see her on the way to school.'

Fran and Edie laughed. 'Then there's hope for Lizzie yet,' Fran said.

Bobby nodded. 'Well yes, there certainly is. You three had better get ready to do your stint on stage. The band has set up and Basil's looking twitchy like he always does just before a show starts.'

'Levi and Dianna are going to sing first, I believe,' Bella said, looking across to the table where her sister and Earl were sitting with the children. Molly was adjusting Dianna's hair and Levi looked thoughtful and smart in his new suit. Her heart filled with pride as she gazed at her son. He was such a handsome boy. 'But first Mam and Martin have to do the first dance. It's traditional.' As she spoke Basil got up on stage and asked the newly-weds to take to the floor for the first dance. As the band struck up with Vera Lynn's wartime sweethearts' favourite tune, 'The Anniversary Waltz', Martin led Mary onto the dance floor. After a few seconds they were joined by other couples.

Bella felt her eyes filling as she looked at her mam gazing into Martin's eyes. She looked so happy tonight and she deserved some time to herself now and to enjoy her new home and life. She'd always been there for her girls and her grandchildren, but she was still young enough to enjoy a long and happy marriage with Martin. Bella smiled to herself, thinking back to the day she'd gone with him to choose the engagement ring. He'd been so excited and he clearly adored her mother, and she knew he'd be a wonderful stepfather to her and Molly.

As Stevie and Edie got up to dance, Bobby tapped Bella on the shoulder. 'Help me up, love. Let's see if I can manage a gentle shuffle.'

'Go on, you two,' Fran said. 'I'll keep an eye on the kids.'

Bella smiled and helped Bobby to his feet. He took her in his arms and they swayed together. It felt good. They often had a little dance in their own sitting room at home, when Bobby's false limb wasn't rubbing the stump of his leg too much and causing him pain. As the song came to an end and the guests clapped, Bella helped Bobby return to his seat.

Basil announced that the evening's entertainment was about to start, and introduced Dianna and Levi as the talented winners of the recent *Carroll Levis Discovery Show*. A huge cheer went up from everyone, including the members of the Wavertree WI who were all guests for the evening.

Levi grinned and bowed and Dianna did a little curtsey. She had already told her dad she was not going to sing any Shirley Temple songs tonight, but Levi said he didn't mind doing one, his favourite, 'On the Good Ship Lollipop', so Dianna stood at the side of the stage as her brother strutted up and down, singing his heart out. As everyone clapped and cheered him, Basil told the audience they would now sing the song that had undoubtedly won them the talent show. Dianna beamed at him and took her place by Levi's side. Levi grinned at her. His favourite song, and he'd done this one for Granny Fen and Uncle Basil on their wedding day, so it was nice to do it for his Granny Mary and Martin tonight. The pair sang 'The Whole World in His Hands' with gusto and as they finished, everyone got to their feet, clapping and cheering.

There was a short break, with the band playing a few Glenn Miller songs quietly while people replenished their drinks. The Bryant Sisters went backstage to get changed into their freshly cleaned and pressed military uniforms.

Then they stood waiting behind the curtains while Basil told a couple of jokes before introducing them, telling the audience that this was the first time they'd sung as a trio in public for some time so they were in for a special treat and to give them a big hand. The girls marched on stage and saluted as the trumpet player, wearing a military cap, signalled the start of 'Boogie Woogie Bugle Boy'. Everyone cheered as they began to sing in perfect harmony. Basil stood in the wings watching them, filled with pride. His girls, his blonde, his brunette and his redhead, all so different, but all so perfect, and their harmonies were astounding. Next they sang 'Rum and Coca-Cola' and then 'Don't Sit Under the Apple Tree', and finished their Andrews Sisters' spot with a tribute to the late Major Glenn Miller with 'Chattanooga Choo Choo'. The audience was on its feet, clapping and cheering and shouting for more.

'You'll get more later,' Basil told them, beaming from ear to ear.

Fran burst into tears as they ran into the makeshift dressing room. 'Give me a group hug, girls, please,' she said as Bella and Edie flung their arms around her. 'I am so glad I came back,' she sobbed. 'I did the right thing, didn't I? This is where I belong, with my best friends and my family.'

Bella felt tears rushing to her eyes. 'You did. And we are so glad you are back.'

'We are,' Edie agreed, dashing a hand across her face to wipe her own tears away. 'We're complete again now. Onwards and upwards, girls.'

At the end of the night, when the girls had finished their final song, Bobby and Bella got up on stage to sing a duet. Bobby announced the song because Bella knew she couldn't do that without bursting into tears.

'This song is dedicated to a little lady who can't be here tonight in person,' Bobby began, 'but I am sure she is with us in spirit to see her mam married to Martin. This one's for you, Betty, sweetheart.' Bella swallowed hard and held Bobby's hand as they sang her little sister's favourite song, 'Over the Rainbow'. She saw Mam and Molly wiping their eyes and blinked hard to stop her own tears blinding her. She wondered what Betty would be like now. Maybe even married with children of her own. She was never far from the family's thoughts even though she'd only been five years old when they'd lost her to diphtheria. Aunty Et was wiping her eyes and Bella waved to her and did her best to smile. She took a deep breath along with her bow at the end, and Bobby held her close as everyone clapped and thanked them.

As the guests began to leave, Bella sought out her mam and Martin, who were waiting for a taxi to take them to the bungalow that was all ready to move into. Tomorrow they were going to drive to Llandudno for a short honeymoon and stay at the Imperial Hotel, where her mam had once taken afternoon tea during wartime, when the ENSA team were performing in the town. Mary also wanted to visit Conwy and the farm she'd been evacuated to with Molly and where Levi had been born. She'd kept in touch by letter with Ruth, the farmer's wife who'd delivered Levi, and Ruth was delighted that they were going to pay her a visit after such a long time. It would be lovely for Mary to see her friend again.

'Mam, have a lovely time,' Bella said, 'and give our love to Ruth and her family. You've got the photos of Levi to show her, haven't you? One day I hope I get the opportunity to take him back to the farm and let her see what a lovely boy he's growing up to be.'

'Yes, love, I've got everything. Now look after one another and we'll see you next week. Keep an eye on our Molly and make sure Dianna's okay too. I worry about her at times. Right, the taxi is here. Goodbye and please thank everyone for coming for me. I did try and go round the tables to speak to them all but I kept getting sidetracked. We've had a lovely day but we're looking forward to putting our feet up now.'

'Well, that's not very romantic, Mary,' Basil said as he and Fenella gave her a hug.

'Oh, get away with you,' she said, laughing. 'Right, we're off. Goodbye, all.'

NINE

Fran unpacked the last of the boxes that her brother Don had retrieved from the unit where her belongings had been stored for the last few years. Most of her things had been thrown away as damp had got into the building and mould had grown on almost everything, ruining things beyond repair. Thank God for Rita and Charlie's more than generous gesture, she thought now. She'd have been sitting on old tea chests and sleeping on camp beds for months without them. Bella and Edie were popping in shortly and then they were all going down to the studios to rehearse for a show they were doing at the local Legion on Saturday night. She took two well-filled cushions from a Lewis's carrier bag and put them on the chairs by the fireplace. Her mam had brought them round first thing on her way to the shops, a little house-warming present, she'd told Fran. The olive-green background and orange and yellow floral design on the covers went well with the green armchairs and mottled green and brown carpet square and really gave the room a stylish finish. It was a room she felt proud of and she couldn't wait to show off her new home to friends and family. When she'd lived across the street with

Frankie she'd always felt guilty about inviting anyone round, as he'd pull his face and tell her to stop wasting time gadding about when she should be doing the housework while he was out at work earning enough to provide for them all. Well, sod him; she was now ready to join the real world and enjoy it to boot.

A bunch of orange and yellow summer flowers sat proudly in a glass vase on the dining table. Fran had bought them yesterday from the flower shop near the park café, and they coincidentally added to the unplanned colour scheme and matched perfectly. The heavy velvet curtains at the window were also olive green and against the cream-painted walls, the room looked smart but cosy. Fran turned on the wireless donated from her brother Don and his wife, just in time for *Housewives' Choice*. She joined in singing along to Jo Stafford's 'You Belong to Me', dancing around the room and swaying her hips. She must remember to remind Basil that this song was perfect for the Bryant Sisters. They had sung it a while back, with Bella taking lead vocals, and now this month it had been released as a record, so she might treat herself next time she was anywhere near Epstein's store in the city. The Jepsons had left her a gramophone in a polished wooden case, along with a few records. It resided in the front room out of Lorraine's sticky-fingered reach.

A knock at the door had her hurrying down the hallway to answer. She threw open the door and let in Bella and Edie. 'Come on in.' She greeted her friends with hugs and kisses and led them through to the back sitting room. 'Let's make the most of the last couple of days of peace before school and nursery finish for the summer holidays.'

'I second that,' Edie said, laughing.

'I third it,' Bella added, rolling her eyes. 'I'm actually dreading it now Mam's moved out. I can't keep dumping Lizzie on her; she needs a break and to enjoy her first few weeks with

Martin in peace. But it means I won't be able to do as much studio work for a while.'

Fran nodded. 'Lorraine will be going to my mam's and I think Edie's arranged for Dennis to go to hers.'

Edie smiled. 'I have. Maybe mine can help you out with Lizzie now and again.'

'That would be lovely, but I don't want to put on her. Lizzie can be quite a handful. She doesn't listen. Everything just goes over her head.'

Fran sighed. 'Well, sit down and I'll pour us a cuppa. It's already brewed in the pot and waiting. I've got some nice custard cream biscuits in as well.'

'When did you last get Lizzie's ears checked?' Edie asked Bella. 'You've mentioned a few times that she doesn't always seem to hear you. It might just be that she's being naughty, but you never know with kiddies.'

'Actually, she's not had her ears checked since she was a baby,' Bella replied. 'I've thought for a while that something wasn't quite right with her, but no one else seems to be concerned. I suppose there's a possibility that she could be slightly deaf, at least. There's no reaction on her face at times when I speak to her, like she simply hasn't heard me. I'll see what Bobby says about it later. He says she's just a pest, but it's certainly something to think about.'

Fran came back into the room with a tray of tea things. 'I overheard what you said about Lizzie's hearing, Bella. On the few times I've seen her, I've also noticed she doesn't always respond when you say something to her, like she's in her own little world at times. I'd definitely think about getting her an appointment to see the doctor.'

Bella nodded her agreement. 'I think I will.'

· · ·

Bella and Bobby sat opposite Doctor Jackson as he explained what he thought the problem might be with Lizzie, who was sitting on Bobby's knee, gazing around the room. Bella had told Bobby she was concerned after the conversation she'd had with Fran and Edie. They'd tried a few tricks on her, including shouting 'Boo' as she'd walked close by. Bobby blew up and popped a balloon behind her and she barely flinched. He'd also banged on Levi's old toy drum and again there had been no response.

Doctor Jackson told them he would arrange for Lizzie to see a hearing specialist at the Royal as soon as possible. He'd tried a few simple tests; he'd placed headphones on her ears and given her a tiny hammer to hold and carefully explained to her, speaking slowly and clearly, to tap the desk each time she heard a noise through them. As the doctor fiddled with the audiology equipment Bella and Bobby could hear the high-pitched squeaky noises even without headphones, but Lizzie just sat still as though in a trance. Not once did she tap the desk with the hammer.

'Until I have a second opinion I can't make a full diagnosis, but I have to tell you that your daughter definitely has some form of hearing loss, Mr and Mrs Harrison. Whether it's permanent or not is impossible for me to say right now. Hopefully we will have an appointment arranged within the next two weeks and we'll take it from there. Meantime, when you speak to her, try and make sure she is facing you and speak slowly and clearly to her face. Most children with a hearing impairment learn to lip-read early on. She probably already recognises certain words and commands from you. Now, I know you will, but do try not to worry. Deaf children learn to adapt and of course there is sign language, which can be taught to Lizzie and yourselves so you can communicate easily with her for the future.'

'Thank you,' Bobby said. 'We'll wait to hear from you and the hospital then.'

He and Bella left the surgery, Lizzie walking between them holding their hands. 'You okay, Bella? You look white as a sheet,' he said.

'I'm just shocked,' she replied as they waited on the corner of Picton Road for Basil to pick them up. 'I knew there was something wrong, but was hoping he'd say it was impacted earwax or something and to drop a bit of warm olive oil or drops of some sort into her ears. It's what Mam used to do when we had earache as kids.'

'Mine too,' Bobby said, giving Bella's hand a reassuring squeeze. 'Well, whatever's wrong, we'll get her sorted. Here's Basil now.' Bobby waved as Basil's bronze Bentley car drew close and pulled up beside them. 'Your mam and Martin will be home tomorrow, so no doubt they'll be calling round and we can tell them what's happening.'

Bobby poured Bella a glass of sherry and himself a whisky as they sat trying to relax in their sitting room. Lizzie and Levi were in bed and Basil and Fenella had gone out for a couple of hours, so they had the house to themselves. He looked at Bella beside him on the sofa. 'Do you think it might be my fault that she's deaf?' he began quietly. 'You know, with all my injury problems internally. My, err, my genetic contribution might not have been of the best quality.'

He looked so pale and worried that Bella's heart went out to him. She put down her glass and took his hand. 'Bobby, no, of course it's not your fault. These things happen. Who knows why? Maybe it's just a blockage or a little growth or something that they might be able to remove in time. Please don't ever blame yourself.'

'Well, whatever it takes or costs we'll do the best we can for her,' he said, his eyes filling. 'I feel awful now for just thinking she was being a pest at times. Her whole little world has been silent for who knows how long and we had no idea. I'm sure it's been a gradual thing. And why the heck did no one at her nursery realise there was a problem?'

Bella shrugged. 'Well, we're her parents and *we* didn't really, until recently. We can't blame others for not seeing what we ourselves missed.'

'Well, whatever it is, she's not going into an institution,' he said. 'We will look after her at home and get someone in to teach her if necessary. We're not sending her away.'

Bella chewed her lip. 'Molly might be able to help us with that. We'll face it when we have to. There's a while yet before she's of school age.'

He nodded. 'Mum and Basil were upset. I don't think they quite knew what to say to us. I just can't work out how not one of us realised she couldn't hear.'

'Well, *we've* known for a while that she was a bit different. Now we've got to come to terms with it and accept it for what it is, instead of just thinking she's naughty and hard work. Now we are aware there is a problem, we can start to move forward, depending on what they say at the hospital. '

Dianna pushed the trolley with Harry sitting in it towards Granny Mary's bungalow. Molly was trying to get on with doing the washing and had asked Dianna to take him for a walk and try to get him to sleep, but first to drop off some magazines she'd finished with at her mother's place. She knocked on the shiny red front door and waited for someone to answer. Granny Mary opened the door a fraction and then, seeing who was knocking, opened it wider, gave her a welcoming smile and stood back to let them into the hallway. Harry had already fallen asleep, so they left him in the hallway in his trolley and went into the cosy kitchen at the rear of the bungalow.

'Sit down, my love,' Mary said, pointing to the table and chairs at the top end of the room. 'I've just taken some scones out of the oven. They're cooling on the rack over there. That was good timing, wasn't it?'

'It certainly was,' Dianna said, loving the fragrant scent of baking, just like in Grammy's kitchen back home. She sat down on one of the chairs and looked around the brightly coloured room. 'This is a lovely kitchen, all homely and nice smells. I love kitchens you can sit in and watch people cooking. Just like my grammy's place. Ours in Victory Street is too small.'

'Ah, that's because they're more like a scullery than a kitchen,' Mary said. 'We don't have a dining room here, just this and a nice sitting room at the front. But it's plenty big enough for me and Martin. The Prince Alfred Road house is like a small mansion, too big at times to keep on top of. I have no idea how Bella is going to cope with it all, as Fenella is rubbish at doing housework. They always had a housekeeper living in and then our Molly took over the job when the old one died. Then I suppose I sort of took over when Molly went to college to train to be a teacher. Lord knows who will do it all now. But that's not my problem.'

Dianna smiled. 'It's time for a bit of space for you now and to take things easier. When Dad and Molly move next month, all being well, Ruby and I can manage to look after the little house on Victory Street between us, I'm sure.'

'Oh, you'll be just fine. No kids to clean up after either. I suppose you've heard about our little Lizzie and that she may be deaf? Such a shame; Bella and Bobby waited a long time for that little girl. They are very upset. Lizzie is fine, she knows nothing different. I don't think she's always been deaf, though, and they did tell them that hearing loss can happen over a period of time. I suppose the hospital might be able to do something to help her get it back once they know what's causing it.'

Dianna nodded. 'I had a friend back home who was deaf

from birth,' she said. 'I was taught sign language so that I could communicate with her; several of our friends learnt as well. We made sure she never got left out of anything and she came everywhere with us. I can help with Lizzie and teach her, if Bobby and Bella would like me to do that.'

Mary's eyes filled. 'Oh, love, that would be marvellous. I'm sure they'd bite your hand off. How very kind of you to offer. They'll be made up.'

Dianna smiled. 'I'm more than happy to do it. Lizzie feels like a little sister to me. I think because she's Levi's little sister we're linked somehow. I can maybe teach Levi too, then he can "talk" to her.'

'You're a blessing, you are, my love. Right, let's get those scones and a cuppa while his little lordship sleeps.'

Dianna smiled. 'Oh, yes please. And there are some magazines that Molly sent under the trolley – don't let me forget to leave them for you before we go.'

Mary poured two mugs of tea and buttered two scones. She placed a little dish of home-made jam on the table and sat down opposite Dianna, pushing her mug and small plate towards her. 'How did you get on with telling your dad you no longer want to sing?' she asked.

Dianna shrugged. 'I haven't really said anything yet. Well, apart from dropping great big whopping hints that I am determined to be a nurse one day. He's got a bee in his bonnet about TV appearances now, maybe next year after the coronation. They've got a big show planned for that and I guess Levi and I will be doing our usual stuff. I'm just hoping my twin cousins will be here by then and I might get to sing with them. But as for the future, well, it's not what I want to do.'

Mary nodded. 'Best get the next twelve months out of the way and see what happens. You'll be busy with schoolwork and so will Levi as he's coming up to eleven at Christmas. Next year he'll be working towards his eleven-plus exam, and he's clever enough to pass it as well and go on to grammar school. Both of you need your education, it's important. Bella always wanted to sing, but she finished school first. Mind you, she had to get a job at Bryant and May match factory, as the war had started and we needed her working. Her dad was sent abroad so it was a hard time financially. But that's how they got their name, you know, the three of them worked there, Edie and Fran too, and the foreman called them the Bryant Sisters because they used to sing to entertain the workers at break time. They were eventually discovered by Basil when they were singing in a local club one night and that's how they ended up working with ENSA.'

'And that's how she met my dad,' Dianna said. 'Over at the Burtonwood camp. He took me to see it one afternoon when he borrowed Basil's car, and told me the tale.'

Mary sighed. 'She did, yes. But we have to look on the bright side of all that. We have our lovely Levi and now your dad is happy and settled with Molly. It's a strange world, but there you go.' She laughed. 'And I feel like I have an extra daughter in you, my love. I'm always here if you need to talk about anything.'

'Thank you,' Dianna said. 'That really does mean a lot to me. A mom and a granny all rolled into one. I love my new family.'

'And we love you, chuck, we love you.'

TEN

Bella took Lizzie's hand as they walked to nursery. They'd just dropped Levi off for the first day of his final year as a primary school pupil. They seemed to be no closer to finding out why Lizzie was deaf. The hospital tests had all been inconclusive; no growths or build-up of hardened wax had been detected. There'd been a promise of her being fitted with hearing aids at her next appointment and she had already been measured for them, but for the moment her daughter seemed to understand what they were saying now that they were taking care to position her right in front of them and get down to her height. And she could talk well enough, but her tone was flatter than a normal child's. Again, Bella was puzzled as to why the family hadn't noticed that for themselves. But Lizzie must have been able to hear people talking at some point in her short life, otherwise how had she learnt to say any words? Her becoming deaf definitely seemed to have been gradual rather than from birth. Although when she thought about it, Bella could recall that often, to gain attention, she would shriek and point rather than actually ask for things. Maybe that was out of frustration. Dianna had been a marvel this summer and had spent many hours at the house with Lizzie, teaching her to sign. She'd looked after her while Bella went to the studios on numerous afternoons as well. She wanted to become a children's nurse eventually, she'd told Bobby and Bella, so getting in some practice with Lizzie was perfect for her.

Lizzie's nursery helper came to greet them in the corridor and her daughter went off quite happily, waving a quick goodbye to her mother. The nursery seemed to be coping okay with her condition, so all Bella could do was keep her fingers crossed. Bobby was still convinced it was his fault their daughter had problems, and Bella wished she could make him believe it wasn't anything to do with his injuries. Hopefully in time he would stop blaming himself.

As Bella stepped out onto the pavement she spotted Edie dragging a reluctant Dennis by the hand.

'Hang on for me,' Edie said as she drew level with Bella.

Bella smiled and waited near the door while Edie pulled her son inside the building. She grinned as several seconds later Edie shot out, cheering.

'Thank God for that,' Edie said. 'Little bugger didn't want to get out of bed this morning.' She linked Bella's arm as they set off. 'Fran's got the kettle on,' she said.

'Good.' Bella sighed. 'I promised our Molly I'd help her with a bit of packing later, so a nice brew now will set me up for that.'

'Is it this week they move?' Edie asked.

'Yes, Friday morning. I said I'd look after Harry as Mam is helping them with the move. They're leaving quite a lot of stuff behind, though, because Ruby will need it.'

'Molly told me that,' Edie said. 'Dianna is definitely staying behind as well?'

'She is, but she'll split her time between Victory Street and Earl and Molly's new place.'

'Any more news on Earl's brother coming yet?' Edie asked as they turned the corner in to Victory Street.

'Yes, all being well they'll be arriving in November, just in time to get settled for Christmas. And also it gives Scotty time to get the girls registered for starting school in the New Year.'

'I hope Scotty and his wife manage to find jobs,' Edie said.

'Ruby says Dolores will have no problem getting a place at the Royal. She's a registered senior midwife. They are desperately short of qualified staff on Maternity, apparently.'

'Oh that's good,' Edie said as they stopped outside Fran's front door. 'Did Earl say Scott was an architect? He'll have no problem finding a job either with all the rebuilding going on in the city.'

'He is,' Bella said, raising her hand to rattle the brass letter box. 'Fingers crossed for him.'

Fran opened the door with a big smile. 'Come on in,' she said, stepping back to make room for them to pass.

Bella pointed to a folded sheet of white paper on the doormat. 'Did you drop something?'

Fran frowned and shook her head. 'No. I picked up the post a few minutes ago and that wasn't there then.' She bent to pick up the paper and carried it through to the back sitting room. She threw it onto the table and dashed into the kitchen to bring a tray of mugs and the cosy-covered teapot through. 'Sit down and I'll grab the biscuits. Sugar and milk's already on the table.'

Bella and Edie took seats and Fran came back with a pink china plate of lemon puffs. She put down the plate, picked up the piece of paper and unfolded it. Her eyes widened and she let out a gasp and flung the paper back down as though it had burned her.

'Fran, what's the matter?' Bella asked.

'Read it,' Fran said, her hands shaking, her face devoid of colour.

Bella picked up the paper, looked at it and passed it to Edie, whose eyes grew wide as she read the scrawled words written in thick black lead pencil.

I'm watching you,
I know your every move.
You belong to me and will never be free.
Keep looking over your shoulder
if you know what's good for you.

'Who the heck sent you that?' Bella exclaimed. 'Can't be you-know-who, he's inside.'

'No idea.' Fran shook her head. 'Who would do this, and why? Whoever it was shoved it through very quietly. I didn't even hear the letter box rattle. Did you two see anyone in the street? It can only have been shoved through the door in the last couple of minutes.'

'There was no one around,' Edie said. 'They must have scarpered pretty quick, whoever it was.'

Fran frowned. 'So whoever posted it either lives close by and got back indoors quickly or they're hiding somewhere.'

'But there's nowhere *to* hide,' Bella said. 'No back ginnels within easy reach or passageways between any of the houses. You have to walk the length of the street either way to get around to the communal backyards.'

'Does that bloke still live on this street that used to be friendly with Frankie, the one that worked down the docks with him?' Bella asked.

Edie shook her head. 'They got rehoused to the new estate at Allerton because they were overcrowded with all the kids they had. They've been gone ages.'

'Hmm, but wasn't his wife very pally with the woman

almost opposite Earl's? To the right side of Fran's old house?' asked Bella. 'Is she still there?'

'I don't know,' Fran replied. 'I've just kept myself to myself since I moved in. Apart from seeing Edie, and Earl's family, I've spoken to no one. But that woman may have seen me here and told her friend, and he could have told her husband, Frankie's mate, who could have then got word to him. It was probably Frankie that told him to write it to put the wind up me, evil git that he is. I'll show this to our Don later and let him take care of it. I will not be frightened out of my own house by anyone, least of all him.'

'I think that woman you mean *is* still there,' Edie said. 'I never have anything to do with her, but I'm sure she is.'

'Hmm,' Fran said. 'Thought as much and I bet they're spying on me.'

'You can always stay at ours if you feel worried,' Bella offered. 'There's plenty of room.'

'Thanks, Bella, and I know I can. It's very kind of you. But I have to stay put and let them report back to Frankie that he's not scaring me away, otherwise I will never be free of him. Christ, we're bloody divorced and he still thinks he owns me. I'm furious rather than scared right now. I feel like going across the street and banging on the door and having a go at them, because you can bet your life both women are in there now twitching their filthy nets to see what I do.'

Edie patted Fran's arm. 'What you need is to meet someone else, someone that will look after you and see him off once and for all. There'll be the right one out there waiting for you, Fran, mark my words.'

Fran half-smiled. 'Well, whoever he is will have a bloody long wait because right now I am more off men than you can ever begin to imagine.'

'That's more like our Fran,' Bella said with a smile. 'But Edie's right. There are a lot of decent blokes around and in our line of work you have a good chance of meeting one sooner rather than later.'

'Bella, shut up and drink your tea,' Fran said, grinning, the colour back in her cheeks now. She picked up the piece of paper, folded it in half lengthways and bent the corners up, making a pointed end. The paper now resembled a plane.

'What are you doing?' Bella asked. 'I thought you were going to show it to your Don.'

'I was, but I've changed my mind. I can remember all the words, so I can tell him what it says, he doesn't need to see it. Come to the door and watch me.'

Bella and Edie frowned as Fran got to her feet. They followed her to the front door, where she marched purposefully across the street and aimed the paper plane so that it landed neatly on the doorstep of the woman suspect. The grubby net curtains twitched, as Fran had known they would. She stuck up two fingers and marched back to her own house, where she slammed the door shut and she, Bella and Edie convulsed with laughter in the hallway.

'That'll show 'em,' Fran said. 'Let the silly cow report *that* to her stupid husband. He can relay it to Frankie if and when he goes to visit him. See how he likes that.'

'I'd be tempted to get your Don to write to Frankie and tell him to back off or else,' Edie said.

Fran shrugged. 'Let's just see if anything else happens first. If it does then I might report the threats to the police.'

'Molly, sit down and let the men do the lifting and shifting,' Mary said, pushing her daughter down onto a dining chair that had just been brought in. 'You shouldn't be carrying anything heavy in your condition.' She was at Molly and Earl's new house on Queen's Drive while the removal men emptied the van of furniture. 'Just give them instructions of where you want things to go.' A delivery van from Lewis's store had also pulled up and two men in brown overalls were bringing in a new three-piece suite and the rest of the dining room furniture. New beds had already been delivered and Earl was upstairs with Martin, putting headboards on the divan bases: a double bed for him and Molly, and a single for when Dianna came to stay. Harry's cot was already in place in the smallest bedroom that overlooked the large garden. 'I'll make a start on unpacking the kitchen boxes and put the pots and pans away in the cupboards,' Mary said. 'Then when they've finished with the beds I'll go and put some bedding on.'

Molly nodded. She looked white-faced with tiredness. 'The new bedding is in bags already in the bedrooms, Mam. You'll find them, there's one in each room with sheets and blankets and everything in. Thank you so much for coming over and helping, I couldn't have managed without you. And thank goodness for our Bella looking after Harry as well. He'd have been a nightmare, into everything.'

By the time Basil and Fenella brought Bella and Harry to the new house the downstairs rooms were beginning to look more like a home. Mary had worked hard, with Molly doing as much as she could without overtiring herself.

'It's very nice, Molly.' Fenella looked around, admiring the light and spacious lounge and dining rooms, with their large bay windows overlooking the gardens. 'Very bright and airy. Just the sort of place I fancy moving to eventually, but without the stairs, if possible.'

'I second that,' said Basil. 'Definitely no stairs next time.'

'You need a bungalow like Mam and Martin,' Bella suggested.

'We do, dear,' Fenella agreed. 'We are going to start looking soon. I've been told there are some new bungalows being built in Woolton, not far from the park and across from the children's home at Strawberry Fields, so we're going to look into it.'

'Woolton's a very nice area,' Mary said, handing round mugs of tea. 'Find a seat wherever you can. Well, if you two leave the big house that just leaves Bobby, Bella and the kids there.'

Bella sighed and flicked her hair back over her shoulders. 'In all fairness, if you go too, then I think Bobby and I should also look at bungalows. He'll do so much better all on one level and we could do without steps out to the garden too.'

Fenella nodded. 'He would, you're right. It would be much easier for him. I think we need to sit down and have a discussion about this soon. My house is paid for, so if we sell and split the money, we will each have a very good deposit to help with buying something else, maybe even be able to buy outright. Also, if we buy new, then we don't have to worry about having any jobs to do on the properties for quite some time.'

'Sounds like a good plan to me,' Basil said. 'Something to definitely think about.'

'Well, that would certainly be the end of an era,' Mary said.

Earl caught the tail end of their conversation as he and Martin came downstairs. 'All finished up there,' he said, accepting the mug of tea Mary handed over. 'Just needs the bedding on. Are you thinking of selling your place, then, Fenella?'

She nodded. 'Eventually, yes.'

'Hmm. Your house is the sort of property my brother would probably like. He's an architect and he loves older buildings. It would give him and his family plenty of space. He bought a three-storey period style house when they moved to New York a few years back but of course he's sold that now, ready for buying a place here. If you can stall your plans for a few more weeks until he arrives in November, that would be great. He'd have plenty of room there for our parents to come and visit from

New Orleans in time, and you have Bobby's downstairs shower room, which would be ideal for them to use as they don't fare too well on stairs either.'

'Sounds like a good plan to me,' Basil said, nodding his head. 'What about you, Fen dear?'

Fenella nodded. 'Sounds absolutely perfect. Obviously the new bungalows won't be ready for a while but if we can find out when and reserve one, and if Scotty likes the house, we can probably have one last Christmas in Wavertree and it will give Bella and Bobby the time to find something suitable as well. Maybe even buy one of the bungalows that we're thinking about. Levi will have almost finished at primary school and Basil could drop him off in the morning for the last few months. I believe there is a primary school close by the new estate for Lizzie to attend. Obviously we'll have to discuss all this with Bobby. It was his late father's family home and the house would be left to him if anything happens to me.'

'Well, Scotty will move in with Ruby on Victory Street for the time being,' Earl said. 'So there's no mad rush. But it might all fall into place quite nicely for everyone.'

Bella smiled. It would be lovely for her and Bobby to have a home that was truly theirs, and so much better for him if he could move about easier and enjoy the garden more too. They'd need three bedrooms, though, with having a mixed family; Levi had his own room now – although occasionally Lizzie would sneak in and curl up with him, which he could cope with for the odd night – but he wouldn't want to share with her all the time now he was getting older.

She had to admit to herself that the Prince Alfred Road house was hard work to look after without her mam there. Keeping on top of the cleaning was a never-ending job. Fenella wasn't a lot of help with housework, but if she went then it would be too much for one person. They'd be better off somewhere on one level and smaller. Hopefully Bobby would agree.

ELEVEN

WAVERTREE, NOVEMBER 1952

'Dianna, honey, are you awake?' Ruby called up the stairs. 'Breakfast is ready. Hurry up or we'll miss our lift to the docks.'

Dianna groaned and rolled over onto her side. She peered at the little clock on her bedside table. It was only seven thirty. Too early to get up. Then she remembered, and sat up, blinking. She rubbed her eyes and yawned. Today was the day her family were arriving in Liverpool. She shot out of bed and pushed her feet into her slippers. The bedroom felt chilly; she shivered and pulled on her warm dressing gown, pulling the cord belt tight around her slim waist.

Downstairs Aunt Ruby had piled a plate high with toast; a dish of butter and a pot of strawberry jam stood side by side. Dianna sat down at the table. Aunt Ruby poured her a mug of coffee from the steaming coffee pot and passed her the milk jug and sugar bowl. Dianna savoured the smell. It made a nice change from all the pots of tea that Molly brewed. Funny how most English people seemed to drink tea except when they went to a café and then they often chose coffee. That Camp stuff in a bottle that Aunt Ruby used to flavour her coffee cakes was all most people seemed to have in their grocery cupboards, so no surprise that they preferred tea. Dianna *did* like tea and for a couple of years after arriving in England she had liked to take it in a fancy patterned china cup with a matching saucer like she assumed all English people did, until she discovered that was mainly in films and novels, and most Liverpudlians she'd met liked a big heavy mug for their brews, nothing as refined as dainty china.

She grinned to herself as she buttered a slice of toast, wondering what Ebony and Tammy would make of Liverpool and its people and customs. One thing she did know – her cousins were no pushovers, so if the louts from school started any funny business they would get what's coming. The twins were sporty; Ebony used to play soccer for the girls' school team and Tammy had taken boxing lessons for a while. They might look feminine, with their mass of rich dark brown curls like her own and slim and dainty figures, but she wouldn't like to get on the wrong side of them. She finished her breakfast and rushed upstairs to get ready, chuckling to herself and hoping for some fun times to come.

'Put something warm on, Dianna,' Aunt Ruby called after her. 'There'll be a cold gale blowing down on that dockside.'

'I will,' she called back. She hurried into the freezing cold bathroom and then into her equally cold bedroom. It was going to be a tight squeeze again in the house, but Aunt Ruby had managed to borrow two camp beds from someone at the Royal for the twins and had fashioned the front room into a makeshift bedroom for them. Her Uncle Scotty and Aunty Dolores would have the double bed in the front bedroom and Aunt Ruby had a small single bed in Harry's old bedroom. She'd insisted that Dianna kept her bedroom, as she now did her homework upstairs there, at the little desk her dad had got for her. It would all do for now, until Uncle Scotty bought a place for his family. There was even talk that he might want to buy the big house that Bobby and his mother were going to sell eventually. If they did there would be loads of bedrooms and maybe she and Aunt Ruby could live there as well. She pulled on a pair of warm black wool slacks and a red fluffy sweater that Molly had knitted for her. Her black ankle boots with a zip up the front would keep her feet cosy over the top of a pair of warm socks. She ran her fingers through her ringlets and let her hair fall down to her shoulders. Checking her appearance in front of the mirror, she smiled at her reflection. Christmas wasn't too far off now and her dad and Uncle Basil had been talking about putting on a festive show at the Empire. With a bit of luck she may get away with just doing one duet with Levi and hopefully be able to sing something more grown-up with her cousins. They had plenty of time to practise; the twins wouldn't be going to school until January so that they could start at the beginning of a fresh term. She could take a tram into the city after school and meet them down at the studio in the late afternoons to rehearse. She'd start to have a think about songs that would suit them, not so much the stuff they'd sung in church, as the songs had to appeal to a Liverpool audience who might not appreciate gospel. Fixing a big smile on her face as a knock sounded at the door, Dianna hurried down the stairs and answered the door to Martin, who had been asked to pick them up for the journey to the docks. 'Morning, Martin,' she greeted him. 'Aunt Ruby, our lift is here.' She grinned as Ruby came hurrying out of the back room looking all flustered.

'Oh I feel so excited,' Ruby said, patting her chest. 'I'm all of a flutter inside. I haven't seen my brother for so long. I can't wait.'

Earl, a heavily pregnant Molly, and young Harry were already waiting at the dockside when Martin dropped Dianna and Ruby off. 'I'll go in the café over there and get a warm drink while you all reunite,' Martin said. 'I'll come back after all the passengers have disembarked and fit as many of you in the car as I can. I guess you borrowed Basil's car, Earl, so we can split the luggage between the boots, and you can fit the rest of the family in and we'll meet you back on Victory Street. Enjoy your reunion.' He hurried off and left them all on the dockside eagerly waiting for the tugboats to sail out to bring the big ship into berth.

Earl gripped Ruby by the shoulders as the two red funnels of the stately vessel came into view through the thick mist shrouding the Mersey. Steam belched upwards, mixing with the mist as horns sounded, letting everyone know she was close.

'This brings back memories of our arrival,' he said, his voice husky with emotion, as Ruby nodded her agreement.

'Do you ever regret it? Leaving America,' she asked him.

'Never, not for a moment,' he said, smiling at Molly, who was standing beside him with Harry in his trolley. 'I wouldn't have met my beautiful wife or have my lovely boys in my life, and the new baby to look forward to, if I hadn't taken the plunge. I've never felt so happy. Oh, I know we get the odd snide comment but it doesn't bother me as much as it used to. I think we got more insults in America about our skin colour than we do here.'

Ruby nodded her agreement. 'I feel more accepted at work here than I did back home. I wouldn't go back to live in the States if you paid me.'

'Well, that's good to hear. Let's hope our brother feels the same way.'

Molly took a deep breath as Earl helped her clamber out of the car outside their old Victory Street home. She placed her hands on her back and grimaced. 'Not now, please,' she muttered.

Martin's car was here and already empty so Dianna, Ruby, the twins and Harry, who had squealed to be with his sister, must be inside the house. She and her large baby bump had been squeezed into the front seat of Basil's car that Earl had borrowed as it was much bigger than their own little car, and Dolores and Scotty had been squashed onto the back seat surrounded by some of the mountain of luggage the family had brought with them. They'd just about managed to squeeze the cases into both car boots and anything else had to travel inside the cars with the passengers.

'You okay, honey?' Earl asked. There were only two more weeks to go before her due date and every time she groaned he was by her side with a look of panic on his face.

'Just a bit uncomfortable,' she replied. 'I keep getting twinges. Don't worry. It's playing football with my bladder so I'd better go straight up to the bathroom before I embarrass myself. Just make an excuse for me and I'll be as quick as I can.' Molly pushed open the front door while the others unloaded the car. She could hear the chatter of the excited girls in the back room, all talking at once. It was wonderful for Dianna to have someone her own age in the family to knock around with, she thought. She was usually surrounded by all the little ones demanding her time and attention. Bella had told Molly how good and patient Dianna was with Lizzie, teaching her sign language. Lizzie now had her hearing aids and seemed to be coping fine. She was definitely a happier child now she could make herself understood by signing and hearing things people said to her properly. Bella and Bobby were hopeful she would be accepted into a normal school environment eventually, as she was doing much better at the nursery. Taking a deep breath, Molly heaved her bulk up the stairs, keeping a firm grip on the handrail.

As she washed and dried her hands and smoothed down her windswept hair, tangled from the strong Mersey breezes, Molly felt a really strong pain around her middle and then became aware of warm liquid trickling down her inner thighs and pooling on the lino by her shoes. She groaned, knowing instantly that her waters had broken. The same thing had happened with Harry, but at least he'd been on time and not two flipping weeks too soon. 'Oh for goodness' sake!' she exclaimed. 'You kids certainly know how to pick your times, don't you?' She walked slowly to the top of the stairs and called for Earl, trying to keep the panic out of her voice. What a way to make a good first impression on your new family, she thought. 'Earl,' she called again, slightly louder. Still no sign of him. Molly felt beads of sweat breaking on her face. Where the heck was he? She bent double as another pain racked her body. Hell, this baby wasn't waiting. She screamed his name at the top of her voice again and Ruby appeared at the bottom of the stairs.

'You okay, Molly? He's just having a cigarette out in the yard with Martin and Scotty. What is it, honey?'

'My waters have gone,' Molly said. 'And ooh, ouch, I'm starting to get pains quite close together.' She gripped her abdomen and gritted her teeth. 'Oh, God, Ruby, I'm so sorry to spoil their homecoming reunion like this.'

'Oh my Lord, Molly child, don't you be sorry, it's not your fault. Let me get Dolores. Thankfully she's a midwife. Stay up there, don't try and come down on your own. Go into Dianna's bedroom and lie on the bed. Take the large towel out of the bathroom with you and I'll get some clean ones out of the airing cupboard.'

Molly did as she was told and heard Ruby calling to Earl, who came hurtling up the stairs, followed by Ruby and Dolores.

'Molly, are you okay, honey?' Earl said, dropping to his knees at the side of the bed and taking her into his arms.

Molly nodded, tears running down her cheeks now. 'I think so. I need to get to the Royal but my case is at home. I wasn't expecting this today.' She cried out as another pain gripped her.

'Of course you weren't, but don't worry,' he said. 'We're all here to look after you.'

Dolores took charge and ushered Earl onto the landing while Ruby helped Molly to get out of her outdoor clothes and underwear and made her comfortable.

'Earl, you need to call Molly's mother and let her know what's happening. Tell her that Martin is on his way to pick her up and bring her here,' Dolores instructed him. 'This baby is coming very soon. Trust you, brother-in-law, to give me a job as soon as I walk through the front door!' she teased, her eyes twinkling. 'Go on, get moving and tell Martin to bring Mary. I'll just pop downstairs, check on the girls and Harry and get some water on the boil. This new little Franklin is not waiting. He or she wants to join the party.'

With a mop of thick dark hair plastered to her head and her big brown eyes staring curiously around the room, Patricia Dolores Ruby Franklin arrived at just after four thirty in the afternoon. Molly and Earl had quickly decided their new daughter should be given the names of her two aunts who had made sure her journey into the world was a safe one.

'Well, little one, I wasn't expecting to be delivering you today,' Dolores said, gazing at her little niece. She started to laugh, a deep throaty chuckle. 'They'll never believe this back home when I write to tell them. Thank goodness it was a straightforward birth. You might have picked your moment to arrive, but you were a dream to deliver, little lady.'

Molly smiled wearily. 'She just didn't want to be left out.'

Mary smiled. 'Well done, love. We'll take Harry home with us tonight, so you don't need to worry about him.'

Molly nodded. 'Thanks, Mam. Well, there you go, Earl.

You've evened up the sides now. Two of each. I think that's quite enough, don't you?'

Earl laughed. 'If you say so, my love. Two beautiful daughters, two handsome sons and the best wife I could wish for. What more do I need? I'm a very lucky guy. I guess we should make a few calls and let everyone know our daughter has arrived. What a day.' He kissed Molly on the forehead while the women set to and made her fresh and comfortable before anyone came to pay them a visit. 'I think maybe we should give the house keys to Scotty and family and do a swap,' he said. 'We can stay here for a few days until you feel well enough to get out of bed and go home.'

Molly nodded her agreement. 'I think that's a good plan. You'll need to go with them, though, to get us some clothes and toiletries. Go and sort it out while I have a much-needed rest and a cuppa.'

TWELVE

CHRISTMAS DAY 1952

Martin and Mary arrived at the Prince Alfred Road house just after eleven on Christmas morning, their car laden with freshly baked bread and mince pies and a turkey from Martin's mate's smallholding that Mary had cooked on a low heat overnight. It was still hot and she would carve it ready for dinner at one o'clock. The whole extended family was coming for dinner and then Ethel, and Bella's friends Fran, Edie and Stevie and their children, for tea. She wasn't quite sure where they would all fit but they'd manage; they always did. It would probably be the last Christmas they would spend in the house, unless Scotty, who was in the throes of negotiating to buy the property from Bobby and Fenella, decided to host future Christmas parties.

Basil and Bella came out to help carry everything inside.

'This all smells gorgeous, Mam,' Bella said, savouring the aroma of fresh baking as she carried laden bags through to the kitchen. 'I've made a start on peeling the spuds and carrots and what have you. We were all up at silly o'clock today with Lizzie shouting for Father Christmas and her presents, and Levi, bless him, doing his best to pretend he still believes for his little sister's sake.'

Basil carefully carried the turkey inside and placed the large greaseproof paper-covered tray on the worktop. 'Smells lovely,' he said. 'Shall I make a start on carving it here? There won't be room to do it on the table when everyone is sitting around it.'

'Yes please,' Mary replied, taking off her coat and scarf. 'Where's Fen?'

'She's gone back to bed for an hour. We were up early with the kiddies and she's not feeling too good.'

'Oh, I hope it's nothing serious.' Mary hung her coat on the back of the pantry door and put on a blue paisley patterned cross-over pinny she took from one of her bags.

Basil sighed. 'I'm glad she's upstairs actually. I could do with talking to you, Mary. I'm a bit worried about her. But I won't stand around doing nothing while you ladies are busy with the vegetables. I'll make a start on the turkey; I can manage two things at once.'

'Which is more than you can say for most fellas,' Bella teased, winking at her mother, who grinned.

'Is the dining room fire lit?' Martin asked.

Basil nodded. 'I did it first thing, but it may need topping up.'

'I'll see to that while you get on with the jobs in here. Where are the kiddies?'

'They're in our sitting room with Bobby, playing one of Levi's new board games,' Bella replied. 'Keeps them out of the way for now. Our Molly can do the tables when she arrives. We've brought the spare one up from the cellar last night. She always makes them look so nice for special occasions.'

'She's made a beautiful Christmas cake to bring over,' Mary said. 'She was finishing icing it the other day when I popped round. Don't know how she's found the time with those two babies, and little Patti is waking up every two hours for a feed. Poor Molly! Good job Harry is an easy little fella to look after.'

'I don't envy her,' Bella said. 'Well, I do in a way, but not really.'

'You've got quite enough on your plate with her little ladyship and Levi,' Mary said. 'Right, let's get cracking and then Basil can get a word in edgeways. If you carve as much of the breast as thinly as you can and then do your best with the legs, Basil. It's got to go a long way. I've brought some sausages over as well and they can go in with the roast potatoes. It's a bit extra meat and I know the little ones would probably prefer sausages to turkey. No point in wasting it.' Mary paused for breath and started working on the sprouts. 'So what is it you're so worried about with Fen, Basil?'

Basil shrugged. 'It's all a bit vague really, but she's been complaining of feeling very tired lately and she's had tingling in her toes, fingers and face. Also she's noticed a change in her vision – things are a bit blurry, the print in books and the newspapers, even when she wears her reading glasses.'

Mary pursed her lips. 'She needs to see a doctor really. As soon as we get Christmas out of the way, make sure she makes an appointment. It could be just that she needs to get her eyes checked at the optician's, but she was complaining of pins and needles in her hands the other day when I came round to help her put the Christmas decorations and tree up. That'll be the tingling feeling, I expect, might be something not right with her circulation.'

Basil nodded thoughtfully and proceeded to carve the turkey. 'I'll see that she *does* make an appointment. I know she's all mithered with the moving, but we've reserved a bungalow as you know and as soon as Scotty gets the go-ahead for buying this place we can start to get prepared to go.'

'She'll be better with less of a house to worry about,' Mary said, 'and so will you and Bobby, love,' she directed at Bella.

'I can't wait, Mam,' Bella said, throwing the potatoes she'd prepared into a large saucepan and filling it with cold water.

'We've already made a start on packing things away that we won't need for a while.'

Martin popped his head around the door. 'Earl and Molly have just pulled up. I'll go and let them in. What time do you want me to go and pick Ethel up, Mary?'

'Oh not until after the princess does her speech, love. About four-ish, then she's here for her tea. She's having her dinner with one of her sons and then he'll walk her home so she can have a bit of a rest before she comes here. I've got her spare key in my purse; remind me to give it to you as she'll no doubt fall asleep and might not hear you knocking. You can let yourself in then and she knows you're coming so she won't be shocked at you walking in on her.'

'Okay, love,' Martin said. 'Be nice to see her again.'

'It will,' Mary agreed. 'It'll seem strange Princess Elizabeth making her first Christmas speech, won't it? I can't call her queen just yet; it doesn't feel right until she's crowned. Oh I know a lot are already doing that, but it's not for me.'

Martin laughed and went to let Molly and family in. Earl carried a child in each arm and Dianna and Molly brought in the food that Molly had prepared for later that day. Dianna put down her parcels and gave everyone a hug.

'Merry Christmas to everyone,' she said. 'Or as we say at home, happy holidays.' She laughed. 'I don't know why I still say "at home"; Liverpool is home now.'

'It's good to see you, Dianna,' Basil said. 'I wasn't sure which house you'd be staying at last night.'

'I decided to stay with Dad and Molly,' she replied. 'I was able to help with the little ones and it was lovely to see Harry all excited with his gifts under the tree this morning.'

'And very grateful we were for your help, honey,' Earl said. 'Where's my boy?' he asked Bella.

'Levi's in the front room with Bobby and Lizzie,' Bella

replied. 'Just go on through. Are you okay carrying those two? Harry looks heavy these days.'

Dianna took hold of her little brother and put him down on the floor. 'He doesn't need to be carried. He can walk just fine.' She took his hand. 'Come on, Harry, let's go find Levi and Lizzie.' Harry beamed as he toddled away with his big sister.

Molly smiled as she unpacked the bags she'd brought in. 'She's so good with the kids. She'll make a great children's nurse one day.' She looked at Earl and shook her head. 'It's what *she* wants. So don't start arguing about it.'

'I wasn't going to,' he said. 'It's Dianna's future. But you gotta admit that she sang real well last night with the twins when they all came round to us.'

Molly nodded. 'She did, you're right. But let it drop now. I want a nice peaceful Christmas Day, the last we'll have here unless Scotty invites us all round next year. And we can have a sing-song later. We always do it at Christmas and Bobby plays piano.' Molly smiled as Earl's face lit up. 'Right, you go and see Levi and I'll make a start on prettying up the tables in the dining room. Are the cloths, napkins and cutlery in there already, Mam?'

'They are, chuck,' Mary replied. 'And the glasses are all set out on two trays on top of the sideboard.' She smiled as Molly waltzed out of the kitchen with a bag of decorative bits and bobs she'd brought that she'd work her magic with. 'Shall I take a cup of tea up to Fenella?' she directed at Basil.

'Yes please, Mary. See what you think when you speak to her. She really doesn't seem right to me and I'm worried about her.'

Mary nodded. 'Well, try not to worry too much.' She filled the kettle and set about making a pot of tea. 'I'll make one for all of us.' She poured a mug for Fenella and left the others to pour their own.

Upstairs, she tapped lightly on the door of the bedroom that

Fenella shared with Basil. Although she was heartened to hear Fenella calling 'Come in,' Mary frowned at the frailness of her voice. She opened the door and popped her head around. 'Brought you a nice cuppa, Fen.'

'Oh thank you. That's very kind of you,' Fenella said, shuffling up against the padded headboard. 'I bet it's chaos downstairs. I'm so sorry I couldn't help you.'

'All under control,' Mary told her, putting the mug down on the bedside table and placing another pillow behind Fenella's head and shoulders. 'Now here you are, drink this while it's nice and hot.'

When Fenella had finished drinking her tea, Mary took the mug from her. 'How are you feeling now?'

'I think I'm okay,' Fenella replied. 'I'll get up in a few minutes and come downstairs to help you.'

Mary put her head on one side. 'You look really pale. Why don't you stay here for now and I'll send Basil up to help you get ready about half an hour before we eat. It's a bit noisy down there now and we don't want you getting all flustered. At least they'll all be quiet when they're eating.'

'Well, if you think you can manage, I will stay here if you don't mind. I don't want to get in the way and hold things up. I wish I knew why I felt so strange. I think I'm going to have to give in and go and see my doctor after the holidays.'

Mary nodded. 'I think you'd be wise. You might be a bit overexerted with all the rushing about at work and the mither about leaving this place after you've been here for so long. It'll be a big change for you.'

Fenella sighed. 'It certainly will, but we'll be better for it in the long run. Basil struggles on the stairs with his breathing. It exerts him too much.'

～

They all took a moment to admire Molly's beautiful table settings of decorated pine cones, red candles, sprigs of fern and holly and red satin ribbon bows, and all the little place-cards with their names on that she'd designed.

'You should go into business, Molly,' Bella said. 'You could do weddings and special occasions. You always do a good job, and look how gorgeous the Christmas cake looks as well.'

Molly laughed. 'I wish I had the time. Maybe when Harry and Patti are older I might think about it.'

'You should, honey,' Earl said. 'We are often asked to supply the music for weddings so along with a band, we can tell them you are available to do the table decorations.'

'Hmm,' Molly said. 'One day maybe. Remind me in a couple of years.'

Bella looked across to where Scotty and his wife Dolores were sitting opposite her and Bobby, and smiled. Scotty was the image of Earl and his wife was a beautiful lady. She was glad they were able to have Earl's family here today. It would be hard for them, thinking of those they'd left behind, especially Earl's elderly parents. She couldn't imagine a Christmas without Mam and Molly. Dianna often talked about her grandparents and how she worried that she might never see them again. She looked happy enough today, though, with her cousins for company. All three girls looked stunning in their red velvet dresses made especially for the holiday season. Last night they'd sung at midnight Mass and Bella had felt shivers run down her spine as their pure voices rang out loud and clear. Hopefully they'd sing later, as was the tradition, with all the family joining in.

Basil brought Fenella down to the dining room and Mary helped her to her seat. She had a little more colour in her face now, thanks to a bit of make-up.

'This all looks wonderful, ladies. What would we do without you?' she said.

Mary smiled. The room did look lovely. The decorations on the Christmas tree in the bay window twinkled as the firelight reflected in the glass baubles, and the pine-scented air mingled with the aromas of roast turkey and stuffing. 'Right, please help yourselves,' she said as she removed the lids from the tureens and dishes. 'Don't be shy.'

Bella helped Levi to fill his plate while Bobby saw to Lizzie, who waved a Christmas cracker in the air. 'Pull it, Daddy,' she said.

Bella smiled at Bobby and mouthed, 'That was clear as day.'

He nodded and helped Lizzie to pull the cracker. She didn't respond to the sound but grabbed the trinket and paper hat as they shot out onto the table. Bobby opened the tissue paper hat and placed it on her head. 'Queen Elizabeth,' he said, using his hands and signing at the same time. Lizzie giggled and patted her red crown.

'Fancy our Lizzie having the same name as the new queen,' Mary said. 'We must make sure we don't miss her first speech on the telly later.'

Basil filled everyone's glass and proposed a toast. 'Raise your glasses to a happy new future for us all. Here's to a fabulous new life in England for Scotty and his family and to the girls settling into school.' Everyone raised their glasses and said, 'Hear, hear.'

At ten minutes to three, the family sat down on the sofas and armchairs in the dining room to watch the royal speech, minus the children, who were all in Bella and Bobby's sitting room playing board games under Dianna's watchful eye. Mary and Fenella dabbed at their eyes as the beautiful Princess Elizabeth addressed the nation from her study at Sandringham. It felt strange not to have the king speaking to them as he'd done for so many years.

Since my accession ten months ago, your loyalty and affection have been an immense support and encouragement. I want to take this Christmas Day, my first opportunity, to thank you with all my heart.

Each Christmas, at this time, my beloved father broadcast a message to his people in all parts of the world. Today I am doing this to you, who are now my people. As he used to do, I am speaking to you from my own home, where I am spending Christmas with my family; and let me say at once how I hope that your children are enjoying themselves as much as mine are on a day which is especially the children's festival, kept in honour of the Child born at Bethlehem nearly two thousand years ago.

Most of you to whom I am speaking will be in your own homes, but I have a special thought for those who are serving their country in distant lands far from their families. Wherever you are, either at home or away, in snow or in sunshine, I give you my affectionate greetings, with every good wish for Christmas and the New Year.

At Christmas our thoughts are always full of our homes and our families. This is the day when members of the same family try to come together, or if separated by distance or events meet in spirit and affection by exchanging greetings.

But we belong, you and I, to a far larger family. We belong, all of us, to the British Commonwealth and Empire, that immense union of nations, with their homes set in all the four corners of the earth. Like our own families, it can be a great power for good – a force which I believe can be of immeasurable benefit to all humanity.

My father, and my grandfather before him, worked all their lives to unite our peoples ever more closely, and to maintain its ideals which were so near to their hearts. I shall strive to carry on their work.

Already you have given me strength to do so. For, since my accession ten months ago, your loyalty and affection have been an immense support and encouragement. I want to take this Christmas Day, my first opportunity, to thank you with all my heart.

Many grave problems and difficulties confront us all, but with a new faith in the old and splendid beliefs given us by our forefathers, and the strength to venture beyond the safeties of the past, I know we shall be worthy of our duty.

Above all, we must keep alive that courageous spirit of adventure that is the finest quality of youth; and by youth I do not just mean those who are young in years; I mean too all those who are young in heart, no matter how old they may be. That spirit still flourishes in this old country and in all the younger countries of our Commonwealth.

On this broad foundation let us set out to build a truer knowledge of ourselves and our fellowmen, to work for tolerance and understanding among the nations and to use the tremendous forces of science and learning for the betterment of man's lot upon this earth.

If we can do these three things with courage, with generosity and with humility, then surely we shall achieve that 'Peace on earth, Goodwill toward men' which is the eternal message of Christmas, and the desire of us all.

At my coronation next June, I shall dedicate myself anew to your service. I shall do so in the presence of a great congregation, drawn from every part of the Commonwealth and Empire, while millions outside Westminster Abbey will hear the promises and the prayers being offered up within its walls, and see much of the ancient ceremony in which kings and queens before me have taken part through century upon century.

You will be keeping it as a holiday; but I want to ask you all, whatever your religion may be, to pray for me on that day – to pray that God may give me wisdom and strength to carry out the solemn promises I shall be making, and that I may faithfully serve Him and you, all the days of my life. May God bless and guide you all through the coming year.

THIRTEEN

As Mary and her daughters finished putting the last of the clean dishes back into the kitchen cupboards and Molly settled Patti down for a sleep in her carrycot, Martin arrived back at the house with Ethel in tow. 'Afternoon, Et. Merry Christmas to you, chuck.' Mary gave her friend a hug and a kiss on the cheek. 'Did you enjoy your dinner with your boys and their families?'

Ethel raised an amused eyebrow. 'It was lovely to see them all, but our Danny's wife isn't the best cook in the world. She did her best I suppose but with every mouthful I kept thinking about your crispy roast potatoes and willing myself to look as though I was enjoying hers.'

Mary laughed. 'What are you like? Well, we've managed to save a bit of turkey for sarnies later on, so at least you'll get a bit of our dinner down you.'

'Don't suppose you saved any potatoes?' Ethel's face held a look of hope.

'I saved you a couple,' Mary said, chuckling. 'Give your coat and scarf to Martin and go and get yourself sat down in the dining room in front of that lovely fire. It's proper nippy when you move away from it. Basil will get you a drink.'

Ethel stuck her head around the dining room door and called out a greeting.

'Ethel, come on in,' Fenella said. 'How lovely to see you again. How are you doing? Are you managing okay now you're back home?'

'I'm doing fine, love, thank you.' Ethel sat down next to Fenella and accepted the schooner of sherry Basil handed to her. She held it aloft. 'Cheers, everybody.'

'Cheers to you too, Ethel,' Earl said. 'Good to see you again.'

'You too, Earl, and it's nice to see your family again. How are you settling in, Scotty?'

'Early days, but we're doing fine,' Scotty replied. 'In fact, we just love it, don't we?' he said to Dolores.

She smiled and nodded her head. 'We do indeed. We're so lucky to be part of this wonderful extended family of Earl's. You've all made us feel so very welcome, right from the start. I can't wait to begin my new job at the Royal next week, and the girls of course will be going to school in January. We're just waiting for Scotty to find something now and we're all set.'

Scotty nodded and continued. 'Hopefully I'll be overseeing our move to this beautiful house in the not-too-distant future, and I may think about starting my own consultancy business. I design buildings you see, preferably houses. If I could team up with a firm of builders we might be able to work alongside each other. I'm busy looking at all angles of that idea for now.'

'Well, living somewhere posh like this house will be right up your street,' Ethel said, and took a sip of her sherry.

Bobby laughed. 'I never really thought of this house as posh, but I suppose it is when you think about it.'

'Well, it is rather grand, Bobby dear,' Fenella said. 'It always feels quite palatial with its high ceilings and cornices, and the Georgian windows are a dream to dress. I shall miss it. But it's just not practical for us any more.'

Bobby nodded. 'I agree, Mum. Bella and I can't wait now to

move to our new bungalow. It will mean I'll actually be able to get into every room in my own home at last. I'll be able to walk out into the garden instead of needing Martin to help me up and down the outside steps. It's freedom in a way and it will feel amazing.'

Bella stroked his arm. 'It will be wonderful for you, for all four of us to have our own home at last.'

'That's the door,' Basil said, rising to his feet as a loud knocking sounded. 'No doubt it's the rest of my lovely girls and their families. I'll go and let them in.' He made his way out to the hall and let in Fran, Edie and Stevie and two excited little ones. 'The kiddies are all in there.' He pointed to Bella and Bobby's room. 'Dianna has got them all organised with her cousins and they're enjoying playing games.'

'Oh, that's good,' Fran said, taking Lorraine's coat and hat off. 'Now be a good girl in there, I'm only down the hall, okay?'

Lorraine nodded and, grabbing Dennis by the hand, she marched him into the room and pushed the door shut.

Fran laughed. 'Well, that was easy. Phew. Come on, you two, let's get in the back room before they come looking for us.'

Edie and Stevie needed no second telling and followed a grinning Basil down the hall to the dining room. They hugged and kissed everyone and accepted the glasses of sherry for Fran and Edie, and whisky for Stevie, that Basil handed them.

'Cheers,' Fran said, raising her glass. 'Merry Christmas to all you English lot and happy holidays to you Yanks.'

Everyone laughed and they all raised their glasses to Fran's toast.

Dianna clapped her hands to gain the attention of her noisy charges. She raised an eyebrow in Tammy's direction as Ebony tried to catch hold of Harry as he hurtled around the room with his new doggy on wheels, crashing into Bobby's desk in the bay window.

Tammy shook her head. 'Can't we take them back to their parents yet? It's not fair that we're stuck with them while they all have a good time.'

Dianna laughed. 'Molly needed a break. She was up twice in the night feeding Patti and then up early this morning making things to bring here. It's good for her to take it easy for a while. She hardly ever gets any time off.'

'Well, Patti is sleeping now, but Harry is like a whirlwind with that dog thing.'

'He sure is,' Ebony said with a laugh. 'He'll tire out soon and with a bit of luck he may have a nap. Which game would you like to play now, Levi?'

'Erm, something easy so that Dennis and Lorraine can play too,' Levi said, looking at the lid of his new games compendium set that Granny Mary and Martin had given him for Christmas. 'What about snakes and ladders? Lizzie knows how to play that game too, don't you?' he said and signed this to his sister, who nodded her head and signed back as well as shouting, 'Yes I do.'

'Well done, Levi, and you too, Lizzie,' Dianna said and signed this to the little girl. Lizzie smiled importantly.

'Levi is really good with Lizzie, isn't he?' Ebony said, smiling at her handsome little cousin, whose brown eyes twinkled in her direction.

'He is,' Dianna agreed. 'He learnt the signing so quickly and he really helps Lizzie a lot to explain things to her parents when they struggle to understand her. They're getting there with the signing but Levi is just brilliant.' She looked up as Basil came into the room.

'Are you all okay, kids?' he asked. 'I've just popped in to see if you'd like a glass of lemonade.'

'Please,' Tammy said. 'I'll come and help you carry them through.'

'Thank you.' Basil smiled. 'We're going to have a sing-song in about an hour's time. Granny Mary is just making some sandwiches and then after we've had those we'll all get together in the dining room. Those that are still awake, that is,' he said, nodding his head towards little Harry, who was now curled up on Ebony's knee, sucking his thumb and struggling to keep his eyes open. 'When he's gone off properly, just pop him onto Bella and Bobby's bed behind that screen over there. Then come and let Molly know and she can wedge him in with some pillows so he doesn't fall out.'

'There's a good programme on at half seven,' Basil said, looking up from the *Radio Times*. 'It's called *Television's Second Christmas Party* and the guests include Arthur Askey, Norman Wisdom, Frankie Howerd and Petula Clark.'

'Oh yes please,' Mary said. 'We'll definitely watch that. If everyone has finished their sandwiches and cake I'll clear the plates away and then we can have a sing-song before it starts. We've got a couple of hours.'

'I'll go and bring the kids in here,' Molly said. 'Harry has no doubt fallen asleep, wherever he's landed by now.'

Basil nodded. 'He was almost away on Ebony's knee when I popped in.'

Molly came back, accompanied by all the young ones minus Harry and Patti.

'Right, girls,' Bobby said as he took his place at the piano. '"White Christmas" to start with?'

'Which girls do you want?' Earl asked. 'The Bryant Sisters or mine and Scotty's three?'

'Do you know the words?' Bobby asked Tammy and Ebony. 'I know Dianna does.'

'Doesn't everyone?' Tammy said with a grin. 'It must be the most popular Christmas song in the USA, in the world, even.'

'Okay then, you three, come on and stand around the piano,' Bobby encouraged.

The girls gathered around him as he played the opening bars and Earl timed them in. Everyone sat quietly, listening with pleasure to the three young voices blending in perfect harmony.

Mary and Ethel wiped their eyes as the song came to an end. 'That was wonderful, girls,' Mary said. 'So very moving. How beautifully you all sang then.'

Earl nodded his agreement. 'Wow, is all I can say. I think we have a new trio here, Basil. What do you reckon?'

'I think you could be right, Earl. Girls, we need to talk in the New Year.'

Tammy and Ebony nodded their agreement, but Dianna shook her head. 'Dad, don't you go getting any big ideas. You know what I want to do, and it's not singing.'

'I *do* know, honey, but you can do both. There's nothing to stop you.'

'No, Dad, I can't. I just wish you'd listen to me. I have to study really hard this year if I want to be a nurse.'

Basil smiled. 'I tell you what, Dianna. A compromise. Just indulge us with one small thing. We want to put on a big show for the Coronation Day celebrations in June. Just say you will do one set of songs with your cousins and maybe one or two songs with Levi, no Shirley Temple for you, and he can do a couple as a solo singer. We won't take up too much of your time with rehearsals, I promise.'

Dianna sighed. How could she refuse? It would be such a special day for the whole country and one she would remember for the rest of her life. It would also be lovely to be a part of the history of the event for the future, and something to tell any children she may have one day. She sighed. 'Okay, but just that one show and *definitely* no Shirley Temple songs. And I'm only saying yes because you asked me so nicely, Uncle Basil.' She looked warningly at her dad, who was just about to say something but then, obviously thinking better of it, closed his mouth and nodded instead.

~

In the week between Christmas and New Year and without telling anyone, Fenella went to see her doctor. She didn't want to worry Basil and Bobby, who were really busy at the agency, booking acts to appear on New Year's Eve at the local pubs and social clubs. Sitting in the surgery explaining her various symptoms to the doctor, she couldn't help but feel silly. Everything she described seemed to sound a bit vague and as though she was making them up.

'And is the tingling sensation that you describe with you permanently, or does it come and go?' Doctor Jones asked.

'All the time now, Doctor,' Fenella replied. 'And I'm just so very tired. I used to be full of energy. I know I'm getting older but I've always kept myself as fit and healthy as possible, until lately.'

Doctor Jones nodded. 'I think we need to get you an appointment at the Royal to see a specialist. They will run a series of tests. I'll try and get you in as soon as I can; it will be after New Year, though, but certainly early January. Just try and get as much rest as you can over the next few days.'

'Thank you. Do you have any idea what might be wrong with me?' Fenella's lips trembled. 'My late mother used to have tingling hands and feet and was constantly tired. We became estranged when I left home, but I do know that she died in her late forties of multiple sclerosis.'

Doctor Jones's lip twitched at that and he made a note of that information. 'Once I have all the results in front of me I can then make a diagnosis. It won't do any good worrying or trying to guess at this stage. Like I say, just try and get as much rest as you can over the next week or so until your appointment is through and we'll take it from there.'

Fenella got slowly to her feet. 'Thank you, Doctor. I'll see you soon.' She left the surgery and decided to walk to Mary's bungalow; it was only a couple of streets away from the surgery and Mary was the only one who knew about her appointment. It wasn't that she didn't want Basil to know, but she knew that he would only worry and he had so much work on this week. She'd do the worrying for both of them until her appointment came through and then she would tell him. She'd want him to go with her in any case as she couldn't face going to the hospital on her own. Her feet were tingling and her legs felt heavy, as though she was wading through treacle, as she trudged up Mary's path and knocked on the red front door. She half-wished she'd had Basil waiting outside the doctor's with the car.

Mary was pleased to see her and invited her inside. 'Oh, Fen. Come on in, love. Go and sit down in front of the fire. You look weary and starved to death,' she said. 'I'll make you a hot drink, get you warmed up a bit.'

Fenella took off her hat and coat and sat down on the sofa in Mary's neat and tidy lounge. Mary came through with a tray of tea things and a couple of slices of left-over Christmas cake. She picked up Fenella's outdoor clothes and took them into the hall to hang on the coat rack.

'Right,' she said, coming back into the room. 'Get that tea down you and then you can tell me how you've gone on at the doctor's.'

Fenella's eyes filled at Mary's no-nonsense approach to kindness. She was so grateful that Mary and her family had come into her life since they'd both been widowed. They'd been a good support to each other, even though they were so different in their approach to life. 'I've got to see a specialist and go for tests to the hospital. Doctor Jones wouldn't speculate at this stage, but he knows about my mother and her multiple sclerosis. I remember her having similar symptoms to mine.'

Mary nodded. 'I'm glad you went, chuck. No point in sitting at home worrying. Did he say how long it will be before you get to see the specialist?'

'He told me very soon after the New Year. As soon as I get word, I'll let you know, and then I'll tell Basil I've got an appointment. I need to rest as much as I can for the time being.'

'No point in worrying him until then, I suppose,' Mary said. 'And you can always talk to me in private if you're concerned about anything meantime.'

'Thanks for your support, Mary, I do appreciate it. Let's try and have just one more New Year celebration before everything changes for us all.'

FOURTEEN

Mary gazed in awe at the tastefully decorated sitting room in the Prince Alfred Road house. The dramatic style and warm rich colours reflected Scotty and Dolores' modern tastes. She had to admit that the overall effect was lovely and welcoming. Scarlet and gold brocade cushions adorned two emerald-green velvet sofas with matching curtains, which created a beautiful contrast against the rich red rug laid in front of the fireplace. The rest of the house was decorated in a similar style throughout. It was certainly a departure from how it had looked when Fenella had lived there. Her pastel curtains and muted sofas had always looked fresh, but there'd been a little bit too much cream around for Mary's tastes. Still, it was what Fenella had liked and she'd been happy enough with it. Now happily settled in her new bungalow with Basil, Fenella was learning to cope with her diagnosis of multiple sclerosis and taking life a bit easier. She was beginning to accept the reality that there were days when her mobility was compromised and she needed a little extra help. Mary went round a couple of days a week to do some of the housework, and Bella had taken on hours on reception at the studio until Emily could find another suitable girl to work alongside her. They were hoping there would be a few applicants with the school leavers next month.

Today the whole extended family was gathered around the television set, at Scotty and Dolores' invitation, to watch the coronation of Queen Elizabeth II. A sumptuous buffet was laid out on the dining table in the back room, and Mary couldn't wait to get stuck into it after the ceremony. She was dying to taste Ruby's famous ginger cake that Levi was always praising. The weather was fine today, so they had walked to the house and on the way she and Martin had commented on how lovely it was that everyone was making an effort. Nearly all the houses sported red, white and blue bunting or Union Jacks on flagpoles in the front gardens. Colourful pictures of the princess and Philip on their wedding day were posted in windows. It was a joy to see such support for the young couple, who, in Mary's opinion, had one heck of a job in front of them, a job that *she* certainly wouldn't fancy doing for a million pounds and a gold clock. God help them both. There was such a sense of excitement from everyone they'd met and spoken to on the way here, all agreeing it was a wonderful thing to look forward to after the sad loss of King George VI last year.

Tonight they were going to the celebratory show that Basil had arranged. He'd been hoping to hire the Empire Theatre as he'd done in the past, but the theatre was closed and all the staff were having the day off, so they'd booked the village hall. It had a good enough stage, with fancy curtains to pull back and forth in between acts, and they'd used the room many times before. In the big main area that was often hired out for weddings, there was a wooden dance floor in front of the stage for those who liked a waltz or two. Square wooden tables and comfortable padded chairs lined the edges of the room. In the corridor behind the stage were two cupboard-like rooms that were used for storage and, occasionally, dressing rooms. Just a shame that the hall held a lot fewer people than Basil would have liked to entertain; but not to worry, Mary thought, them that had bought tickets would have a good night and the WI ladies were seeing to refreshments for the interval. A party was to be held on the park this afternoon for the nearby streets, and everyone was helping by bringing a contribution of food to share out. The decorated trestle tables were already set up ready and waiting. Mary knew it would be a day to remember for the rest of her life.

Mary turned her attention to the TV screen as orchestral music filled cavernous Westminster Abbey while dignitaries and guests took their seats. She held her breath as Princess Elizabeth arrived at the abbey, wearing a stunning gown that had reportedly taken eight months to research, design and create – according to Fenella, who had read this information in a magazine article a few weeks ago. The royal dressmaker Norman Hartnell had designed the beautiful dress, and the ivory satin fabric was richly embellished with silver and gold threads and precious stones.

'Isn't the dress gorgeous?' Fenella said to Mary as all the women in the room oohed and aahed their agreement. 'And they have hand-embroidered emblems of Scotland, Ireland, Wales and Canada on the skirt panels. I love that little velvet cape affair she's wearing on her shoulders; it looks like it's attached to the gown itself. I bet that fur is ermine that they've trimmed it with.'

Basil handed out glasses of champagne as 'God Save the Queen' blasted from the TV speakers. He helped Fenella to her feet and they all stood and raised their glasses as they joined in with singing the national anthem. Mary felt moved to tears as she felt hope really was on the horizon at last. After all they'd been through, she and Fenella both losing their dearly loved husbands, losing her little daughter Betty, Bobby with his internal injuries and losing half his leg, the terrible shortages that had led to rationing for many years, the nightly raids on

Liverpool city centre and the many lives lost in the tightly packed residential areas down by the docks. She sighed, wondering how the new queen would cope with the enormity of the task that lay in front of her and still be a mother to her two little children. Charles wasn't five until November and little Anne was not even three. They were only babies. As the ceremony finished with Elgar's 'Pomp and Circumstance March', Ruby and Dolores handed round plates of sandwiches and sausage rolls.

'There's more food in the dining room,' Ruby announced. 'Please do help yourselves. Basil is in charge of the drinks as he always does such a good job, so when you need a refill, just ask him,' she said with a smile in Basil's direction. 'May I just say that you guys in this country sure know how to put on a show. That was quite spectacular and very moving. What a beautiful young lady your new queen is. Such a credit to her late father and this wonderful country. It makes me feel very proud to live here.'

'Ruby, that's a lovely thing to say,' Basil said. 'And we in turn are proud to have you all here.'

'Thank you, Basil,' Ruby said. 'Now all of you, please just tuck in. That food needs to be eaten. The children are making short work of the sausage rolls.' She laughed and turned to her sister-in-law, who was dabbing at her eyes with a handkerchief. 'You okay, Dolores?'

'I'm just fine, thank you, Ruby. I feel so emotional that we are here and witnessing a wonderful part of history first-hand, instead of reading about it in the *New York Times* tomorrow. It's something I will never forget as long as I live. I'm so looking forward to the rest of the day and the show tonight. The girls are so excited, even Dianna.'

Fenella smiled. 'You have made the house look so beautiful, Dolores. I love your colour schemes – so wonderfully vibrant.'

'Thank you so much, Fenella. I love our new home. It's very

like the period style house we sold in New York. Tall and elegant with three floors, and beautiful big Georgian windows that I've so enjoyed dressing. I love sewing and I like to make my own soft furnishings. Even the cushions were made by me.' Dolores' delight in her new home was evident from the excited smile on her face, Mary thought. 'I'm so glad you like what we've done,' she went on, 'because I know how hard it can be to see your old home looking completely different. I think the vibrant colours are a nod-back to my South African parents' heritage. My mother used to love bright colours in the home and she always wore colourful clothes too.' She waved her hand in the direction of a group of framed photographs on a polished mahogany sideboard. 'My family – no missing my mother centre stage in them all, she's the lady with the big smile, wearing the brightest of dresses and scarves.'

'She looks beautiful. What a wonderful smile she has. I actually think the colours here are making me feel a bit livelier than I normally do lately,' Fenella said, her eyes brightening as she looked around. 'I think we should buy ourselves some red cushions, Basil.'

Basil smiled. 'Whatever you say, Fen dear. If it helps you feel livelier, then red cushions it will be.' He dropped a kiss on her cheek and she smiled back at him.

Dianna and her cousins stood nervously behind the curtains as Basil announced to the audience that three special young ladies from America were going to entertain them tonight. Loud cheers erupted and Dianna smiled. Billed as the Franklins, they were to sing three songs. They'd been rehearsing as much as they could in the last few months, although occasionally Dianna had to drop out as she was in the middle of taking her GCE O level exams, the results of which she would know at the end of next week. Something else to feel nervous about. Her dad had suggested a few fancy names for the trio, but Dianna had told him the Franklins would do for now. He'd reluctantly agreed but had said that if they ever did decide to make a career on stage they needed something that sounded a bit more show-business.

'Are you two ready?' she asked her cousins, who were shivering with excitement.

'As we'll ever be,' Ebony replied, clutching Tammy by the hand. Tammy nodded.

The three girls ran on stage and took a bow. The band struck up the opening chords to Frankie Laine's powerful ballad 'I Believe'. The audience fell silent as the trio's voices soared in perfect harmony. They finished the song to rapturous applause and Dianna thanked the audience and announced their next song would be Perry Como's 'Don't Let the Stars Get in Your Eyes'.

Dianna felt herself relaxing and actually enjoying singing with her cousins. Maybe her dad was right and she could do both: nursing for a career, and singing as a bit of a hobby. She'd have to see what the next twelve months brought. Tammy and Ebony had another year at school anyway, so she had plenty of time to work out where her future plans would take her. The trio finished their set with one of the most popular songs of the year, Jo Stafford's 'You Belong to Me'. During rehearsals at the studio Fran had asked Basil if the Bryant Sisters could sing it instead, but he'd told her they were just doing their Andrews Sisters set today and had given the song to Dianna and the girls. There had been some mild grumblings from Fran, as it was her current favourite song, but in the end she had wished them well. Dianna and the twins took a triumphant bow as the audience cheered and clapped. She felt pleased with the way they'd sung the song and the ending felt really emotional; she thought of all the sweethearts in the world who were separated right now for whatever reason. The adrenaline rushed through her veins as Basil whistled from backstage and applauded them as they made their way towards him.

'Well done, girls,' Earl said, giving them all a big hug. 'You did well tonight. I feel so proud of you.'

'Thanks, Uncle Earl,' Tammy said. 'I really enjoyed myself.'

'You girls will go far, mark my words.'

Dianna raised an eyebrow in her father's direction as she followed her cousins into the dressing room to change. Once inside, she took a moment to drink a glass of water as she waited for her heartbeat to return to normal. She had to admit, as she gazed in the large wall mirror at her reflection and the perfectly fitted, jade-green stage dresses that had been made especially by Aunt Dolores and Ruby for the performance that evening, that they all looked classy, and she felt like a star. There was no doubt about it, that really was a fine feeling.

On the morning they were due to receive their GCE exam results, Dianna met Sally on the corner of Victory Street. They rushed excitedly towards one another, linked arms and strolled towards The Mystery Park, where they had arranged to meet some of the other girls from school. Since the coronation show at the village hall, Dianna's popularity had soared among her fellow classmates. Their friends were waiting by the swing park and they all hugged and sang songs as they made their way into the playground.

'I feel sick,' Dianna whispered to Sally. 'What if I've failed them all?'

Sally squeezed her arm and smiled. 'You won't have, Di. And anyway there's always that entrance exam that the hospital runs. You can always take that to get you into the training school. Have faith.'

Dianna sighed. She really didn't want to do the hospital

exams as she'd heard that some people thought they were a second-best way of entering nursing. It would take ages to apply and be accepted if she didn't get the pass marks this time around.

As they all crowded round in the school's main hall with its lingering odour of sweaty gym mats, carbolic soap and boiled cabbage, where they had taken their exams, names were called out in alphabetical order and envelopes handed out. Dianna received hers and went to sit on a chair at the side to wait for Sally. She looked around at the girls still waiting, nervously chewing their fingernails and fidgeting. As Sally turned towards her, excitedly waving an envelope, Dianna smiled and waved back. They sat side by side and counted to three. Both opened their envelopes at the same time, and squealed together.

'I don't believe it,' Sally exclaimed. 'I got the grades I need! Better in fact!'

'So did I,' Dianna said, tears running down her cheeks. She couldn't quite believe it. 'Nursing school here we come, Sal.'

FIFTEEN

Dianna took a final look around her tidy bedroom at her dad and Molly's house to make sure she'd left nothing behind. She fastened up her small brown leather suitcase that her dad had bought her and lifted it down off the bed. She'd decided to spend most of the school summer holidays here with her dad's family, and because of this Aunt Ruby had made a decision to vacate the Victory Street house and had moved in with Scotty and family. After a lovely few relaxing weeks of nice sunny days, with little rain for a change, enjoying trips to New Brighton on the ferry with her cousins and a few days spent at Formby beach with Molly and the little ones, Dianna was about to leave home and start her cadet nurse training alongside her best friend Sally. Neither girl could believe they'd been accepted onto the same course. Both would be resident at the nurses' home at the Royal Liverpool Hospital for the next two years, and then if they passed their final exams, from the age of eighteen they would go on to do another three years' training to become state registered nurses.

'Come in,' Dianna called as someone knocked on her door.

Her dad popped his head inside. 'You ready, darlin'?'

She nodded. 'I think I am. Shall we go? We have to pick Sally up, don't forget.' Sally's family didn't own a car, so Earl had offered to take her to the hospital.

He nodded. 'I know.' He picked up her suitcase. 'Molly and the kids are in the lounge waiting to say goodbye,' he said, his voice husky with emotion.

'Dad, I'm only going to the city. It's not far. You'll see plenty of me when I get days off.'

'I'm sure we will,' he said. 'I just missed years of you growing up when I was away during the war, and now that you are, I don't want to let you go...' He finished, a catch in his voice. 'But you have to carve your own future and this is what you chose. I'm real proud of you, Dianna and I love you so much, never forget that, my firstborn princess.' He put his arms around her and hugged her tight. Their salty tears mingled on their cheeks.

She almost changed her mind at that moment, but then she took a deep breath and smiled. 'Come on, Dad, I'll be back to see you before you know it. You've got Levi and the twins to coach for the Christmas show at the Empire and maybe, just maybe, I will sing one song with them.'

'You know we would love that,' he said. He picked up her suitcase and grinned. 'Come on; let's get you started on the next chapter of your life.'

Dianna and Sally said goodbye to Earl as he helped them into the reception area of the nurses' home with their suitcases. They were met by a stern-faced home sister, who was wearing a calf-length navy blue fitted dress and a starched white cotton cap trimmed with white lace, and shown to their respective rooms, which were thankfully next door to each other on the ground floor's long main corridor. Dianna gazed around her small but comfortably furnished white-painted room with its dark green curtains, matching plain carpet and light green damask cotton bedspread neatly folded on the narrow single bed. An old two-door wardrobe graced one wall, with a nearly-matching four-drawer chest standing next to it, as well as a small bookcase alongside. A white porcelain washbasin with a mirror above and a towel rail underneath stood adjacent to the window. Dianna stepped towards the bed, picking up the white cotton drawstring bag that had been placed on top of the pillow. To her surprise and delight, she saw her name neatly embroidered in red on the top right-hand corner. Inside, she found her cadet uniform, three white cotton dresses, along with a note to say the bag was to be used as a laundry bag for dirty uniforms. Carefully, Dianna removed the dresses, the same as were worn by all cadets in training, and put them on hangers and the four white starched aprons and caps in a drawer, along with her white elasticated belt.

She unpacked her suitcase and put her own clothes away. The night before, Molly had given her a recent family photograph. It was not a farewell gift, Molly had said firmly as Dianna untied the string and unwrapped the brown paper, but a present with a promise to 'see you soon'. Dianna placed the photograph in its elegant silver frame on her bedside table, and smiled as she looked at her brothers and little sister standing next to her. Levi had grown so tall these last few months; he was now almost up to her shoulders. Dianna remembered how she'd felt so jealous at first when her dad had told her that she had a younger brother in England who he wanted to visit. Then when he'd announced they were going to live in Liverpool, she'd been convinced that he would choose Levi as his favourite child. She'd also hated the thoughts of leaving her grammy's lovely cosy home with the handmade quilts on the beds and always the welcoming scent of a fresh cake baked daily. The only home she'd ever felt safe in. But she knew now that her dad had no favourites; he loved all four of his children equally and she'd never felt anything *but* safe in their new Liverpool home. She still half-wished that she could have followed the path he'd chosen for her, and be the singing star he was convinced she could be. But she was glad he had allowed her to forge her own path. He hadn't stood in her way, but instead had put his own feelings aside and allowed her to follow her dreams. She smiled as she took in the details of her new home; only time would tell if she'd made the right choice. A knock on the door, and Sally popping her head inside with a big smile on her face, took her out of her reverie.

'Are you all unpacked?' Sally asked, shaking her brown hair from out of her blue eyes and flicking the length back over her shoulders. 'Home Sister said tea was being served in the dining room from five o'clock onwards. It's gone five now. I'm starving. Shall we go and see what's on offer? I could eat a scabby horse between two bread vans, as me dad would say.'

'That's funny.' Dianna laughed. 'What's *your* room like?'

Sally shrugged. 'Much the same as this one. I think they're rather fond of the colour green. It's a bit prison-like, isn't it? But at least there are no bars on the windows.' She grinned. 'I tell you what, though, this is the first time since I was born that I have a bed, never mind a room, all to myself. And that's pure luxury for me! No more cold feet in me back in the winter, or kids crying for the lavvy at three in the morning. Bliss.'

Dianna nodded, although she couldn't imagine waking up to such chaos every morning. Apart from sharing with Aunt Ruby for a time at Victory Street, she'd always had her own room and had never had to share a bed, even when she'd lived with her mom. She thought of everything her dad had done to provide for her up until now, and realised how very lucky she was. 'Let's go then. I'm hungry too.'

· · ·

The following morning Dianna and Sally joined the rest of the latest cadet intake in the hall for an induction at the Preliminary Training School. There were twelve girls in all and Dianna saw a few nervous faces among them. Matron and Sister Tutor read out the rules and regulations to the assembled new students.

Sister Tutor consulted the sheaf of papers she was holding and glanced at the girls. Her icy blue eyes narrowed and she stared down her long thin nose, looking, Dianna thought, for all the world like she'd encountered a bad smell. Her pinched lips parted to make an announcement.

'Welcome to your cadet nursing course,' she began in a loud, high-pitched voice. 'You will all report for duty on your assigned wards at eight o'clock sharp tomorrow morning, when you will be given a variety of practical tasks to perform until midday.' Her thin lips almost vanished as she pursed them further. 'Following lunch you will assemble here in the training school at one o'clock for theory and human biology lessons that will add to what you have already been taught at school prior to taking your Biology GCE O level. I will hand out envelopes in a moment containing information of your appointed wards. You will have two months initially on these wards and then you will be moved around so that by the end of your course you will have had a good grounding on each ward in the hospital. Following your two-year cadet training, and *if* you pass all the exams, both practical and theoretical, you will then be invited to apply for a place on our state registered nursing course, which will last three years. We expect our nurses to remain unmarried during these five years in total. Any nurse finding themselves in a position where they wish to get married will be asked to leave with immediate effect.' She took a deep breath, glanced back down at her paperwork and continued. 'No boys or men are allowed inside the nurses' home. Any nurse found breaking the rules will be immediately dismissed. Now all that remains to be said is that we wish all of you the very best of luck and hope that you enjoy your training. Remember, the more effort you put into this course, the more you will gain from it. You do, of course, have the rest of today free, but I would suggest that you make a point of searching out your wards so that you will know where to go tomorrow morning. Lateness will not be tolerated. If you'll form an orderly queue at my desk over there I will hand out your ward assignment envelopes.'

Sally squeezed Dianna's arm as they made their way across the large room to the desk under a window. 'She's a barrel of laughs, isn't she?' she whispered.

Dianna nodded. 'You're not kidding.'

'Five years, though, when we are not allowed to marry, or anything,' Sally said as they joined the queue. 'We'll be dead old by the time we've finished! There'll be no decent lads left by then. We'll be old maids on the shelf.'

Dianna stifled a giggle. 'We'll only be twenty-one and at least we'll be qualified to do something maybe later, if we decide to take a break for a few years. My Aunt Ruby has never married, but Aunt Dolores did. She trained first, then married Uncle Scotty and then went back to do midwifery after the twins started school, so all is not lost. And they didn't say we're not allowed to ever go out with boys at all.'

Bella placed the last book and boxed game on the shelf in Levi's bedroom. She breathed a sigh of relief, feeling a sense of achievement. Finally, she'd finished unpacking everything they'd brought from the big house. It had taken ages to get everything done. Life was so busy at the moment, what with her working part-time at the studios and spending her evenings singing with the Bryant Sisters in a few local clubs, not to mention seeing to the kids, as well as taking her turn to help her mam look after Fenella – who had sadly been having some really bad days lately. However, she knew she had nothing really to complain about. Their new bungalow was a joy to live in, and easy enough to look after. Bobby loved the new-found freedom it gave him just to be able to wander in and out of the garden without help. He had turned out to be quite the deft hand with gloves and a trowel. Martin had helped him build some raised flower beds and he'd enjoyed planting a variety of bulbs that would flower next spring.

Levi had settled well at Quarry Bank High School for boys in nearby Allerton after passing his eleven-plus exam. He was enjoying his days there and making friends easily. He'd met a couple of lads the same age as he who were learning to play guitar and had asked Bella if he could maybe have a second-hand one for Christmas.

Woolton Primary School had only accepted Lizzie as a pupil on a trial basis, due to her hearing problems, but so far so good; Lizzie seemed to be coping well. Lip-reading, as well as signing, she had taken in her stride. It all seemed to be second nature to her. She was a lot happier now that she could under-stand things and didn't need to scream and shriek to make everyone know what she was trying to say to them.

Dianna had a free night from her training schedule and was coming for tea, much to Levi and Lizzie's delight. She was a month into her cadet nurse training now and she seemed to be enjoying it. Bella checked her watch. If she hurried, she would catch the butcher's before they closed for lunchtime. Then she was going to pop in to see if Fenella needed anything. Bella usually made her a bit of lunch if her mam Mary wasn't already there to do it. The new girl they'd taken on at the studio seemed to be fitting in well and was getting along fine with Emily, who'd agreed she was the best of the five school leavers who'd applied for the job of receptionist. Clara was a no-nonsense type of girl, but had a great sense of humour, which was essential when working with a bunch of musicians. In her interview she'd told them she was the only girl of her Irish parents, in between five brothers, so she was 'used to silly male jokers as she was surrounded by eejits', as she called them.

Bella put on her warm wool jacket and picked up a shopping bag. She let herself out of the bungalow and locked the door behind her. The day was pleasant, but she had definitely noticed a chill in the air as autumn began to set in. She missed The Mystery Park opposite their old Prince Alfred Road home, and the colourful falling leaves that Lizzie and Levi used to love running through as they crunched under their wellies. Still, they had nearby Woolton Woods to go walking in. She wished the bungalow was a short walk to Fran and Edie's place, as she was seeing less of them since the move. She saw them a few times a week at work, of course, but there was no popping into each other's houses in the mornings for a brew and a catch-up like she'd been used to. Bobby and Basil had told her she should learn to drive. She was thinking about it, as she knew Bobby would never be able to; it made sense that she should learn and then they could do more family things together instead of having to rely on lifts everywhere from Martin or Basil. The garage attached to the bungalow had been developed into an extra room that Bobby was using as a music room to teach piano lessons in at the weekend, but there was a drive to the front of the property so there was plenty of room to park a car.

White's, the butcher's shop, was quite crowded when Bella took her ticket from the counter and found a place in the queue. She had found herself doing much more cooking than she was used to since they'd all moved on. Bella knew she wasn't a patch on her mam or Molly, but she did her best and no one was starving. Tonight she was planning to make sausage and mash for Dianna and the kids, and liver and onions for her and Bobby. As the queue thinned out the butcher's wife smiled and took Bella's order.

'How's Bobby's mam keeping, chuck?' Mrs White asked, wrapping the sausages in greaseproof paper.

'Not too great at the moment,' Bella replied. 'She's so used to being busy and independent and rushing around everywhere. Being stuck at home a lot is taking some getting used to.'

Mrs White nodded sympathetically. 'I can imagine. Oh I know I say many a time that I'd love to stay at home with my feet up all day, but when it's forced upon you, it's a different matter. Give her my love if you're popping in to see her.'

'I will do. I'm on my way there now. Actually, have you got any boiled ham? I can make her a nice sandwich then, it's her favourite and she'll enjoy that.'

'We have. Just in and it's lovely and lean. Will a quarter do you?'

Bella nodded, paid for her purchases, said her goodbyes and made her way to the bakery two doors down. 'Four white rolls please, and two vanilla slices,' she said to the girl behind the counter. Fenella would enjoy her favourite cake as well as her sandwich. *It will cheer her up a bit.* She might as well have a bite to eat with Fenella while she was at the bungalow and before she went home to make tea for everyone.

Basil's car was on the drive and the front door stood open. Bella hurried inside, frowning. It was unusual for the door to be left wide open, and for Basil to be home at this time of day. 'Only me,' she called, a sinking feeling in her stomach as she walked through to the lounge at the back. 'Everything okay? The door's wide open.'

'In here, Bella,' Basil called from the bedroom at the front, his voice sounding anxious.

Bella put down her shopping bag on the kitchen table and dashed into the bedroom, where a pale-faced Fenella was lying on the bed. 'Has something happened?'

He nodded. 'The window cleaner alerted the next-door neighbour. Fen was on the floor and couldn't get up; she managed to attract his attention. The neighbour called me at work and I arrived ten minutes ago. She says she had a dizzy spell and thinks she lost consciousness. I want to get the doctor to visit but she won't let me. Will you talk some sense into her, Bella, while I make her a cup of tea?'

'Of course.' Bella rolled her eyes. 'Well, at least I'll try. I've just brought something in for her lunch. Would you like a ham sandwich, Basil?'

'I wouldn't mind, love, thanks.' He hurried away and Bella sat down on the edge of the bed.

She took Fenella's cold hand in hers. 'You know, it would be best if you let the doctor come out to have a look at you,' she said gently, trying to keep the panic from her voice. Her mother-in-law looked far from right. She wasn't always the easiest woman to get along with, but today she looked vulnerable and frightened, and Bella's heart went out to her.

Fenella sighed and shrugged her shoulders. 'I'm okay. I haven't had any breakfast as I wasn't hungry. It's just a bit of light-headedness. It'll go away when I've eaten something, I'm sure.'

Bella shook her head. 'Maybe. We'll have to see.' She wasn't totally convinced, but she knew better than to try to make her mother-in-law do something if she didn't want to. Fenella was stubborn at the best of times, but she looked so frail these days, a far cry from the strong independent woman she used to be. She was always the one in control and giving orders. It had been sad to see her decline so quickly since her diagnosis. 'I'm going into the kitchen now to make us some lunch and then we'll see how you are afterwards,' Bella said. 'Just stay there for now and rest and Basil will come and help you to the table when it's ready.'

Fenella closed her eyes as Bella pulled the bedroom door closed behind her. She joined Basil in the kitchen. He was standing with his back to her at the worktop, his shoulders hunched and shaking. 'Basil,' she said softly. 'Are you okay?'

He turned to face her, his blue eyes filled with tears. 'I'm so worried about her. She really does need someone here twenty-four-seven now, don't you agree? I don't think we can cope on our own any more.'

Bella nodded. Her father-in-law suddenly looked very vulnerable. She'd never seen him look so lost before. He'd always been the big, strong, much-adored father-figure to her and Bobby following the loss of their own fathers. Always the problem-solver, the one they had all looked up to, for so many years. She realised now that she and Bobby would need to become the stronger pair and step in to help their parents as they got older. 'I do agree. She does. But you know what she says about not wanting strangers coming in and out, she's said it often enough. Basil, I've got an idea that might help us all. Why don't you just work part time at the studios now? It would do *you* good to be resting a bit more as well. Just go into the studio for a couple of hours in the afternoon and me and Mam will pop over, we'll take it in turns each day. That way Fen has always got you here to help her get washed and dressed and see to her personal needs each morning. And she won't be alone for too long when you leave before one of us comes in. Earl and Bobby can manage the business and the girls are both really good on reception. Me, Fran and Edie will do our bit down there at the studios as and when we can too. We'll manage, Basil. You've got to put Fenella first now and look after your own health as well.'

Basil smiled. 'You're a good daughter-in-law, Bella. I don't know what we'd do without you.'

∿

'I'm getting a guitar soon,' an excited Levi told Dianna as the family sat around the table eating tea.

'Err, excuse me,' Bella interrupted, before Dianna had a

chance to reply. 'We haven't actually said you can have one yet, young man. Depends on how well you behave between now and Christmas week.'

'Well, Dad said he'd get me one, didn't you, Dad?' Levi aimed at Bobby. 'And if you two say no then I'm sure my other dad will say yes.'

Bella bit her lip and took a deep breath. Levi was getting to be a bit cheeky since he'd changed school, but she supposed, or rather she hoped, it was all part of growing up and trying to be one of the boys. He'd always been such a good child, polite and done exactly as he'd been told, but there was definitely a change in his attitude lately. She'd love to know who he was mixing with at school. Maybe it would be wise to get him to bring some of his friends over for tea one day – although thinking about it, maybe that was more a primary school thing. She might suggest the idea later when Dianna had gone back to the nurses' home, see what he thought. Perhaps he was just showing off in front of her.

'Actually I *did* say he could have one for his birthday,' Bobby admitted a bit sheepishly. 'He's helped me in the garden a lot and it's a thank-you for that really. Also, selfishly, I was so pleased when he said that he wanted to learn. Music could be something that me and him could do together, particularly as he gets older. One of our guitarists would come over and give him some lessons. It's good for his future to play as many instruments as he's willing to learn. He'll pick it up so quickly. He's brilliant at playing the piano; he learnt that easily, as you know.'

Dianna laughed. 'Looks like you're outnumbered, Bella,' she said, adding, 'Dad also said he should learn.'

Bella rolled her eyes. 'Looks like I am. Anyway, never mind him and his guitar for now.' She smiled at Levi, who gave her his wide cheeky grin in return, his big dark eyes twinkling. 'How's the training going, Dianna? Are you enjoying it?'

Dianna nodded. 'Yes, it's okay. I knew it was going to be a

steep learning curve, but it's even harder work than I thought it would be. It can be messy and smelly at times as well.' She wrinkled her pert little nose. 'They seem to delight in giving us cadets the worst jobs: cleaning grotty dentures.' She smirked. 'That's a new word I picked up from some of the other girls – emptying and washing bedpans, changing messy beds. It all makes me gag. I spend half my morning trying not to throw up in the sluice.'

Dianna sighed. Life at the Royal was certainly nothing like the *City Hospital* TV show she'd watched back home, she thought, where the nurses were always glamorous with spotless white aprons and the doctors were all young and dishy, a far cry from some of the bewhiskered and grumpy older doctors that walked the halls of Liverpool Royal. 'Then there's all the studying we have to do after our shifts as well,' she went on. 'I feel very tired some nights and fit for nothing.'

Seeing the look on Bobby's face, she realised that she was painting a rather bleak picture, and made an effort to change her tune.

'I love the social side of things though,' she said quickly. 'We don't have a lot of free time, but it's great living with the other girls, and I've made some very nice friends. Sally really enjoys it all; the horrible smells don't seem to bother her and she loves having her own room at last.'

Bella laughed. 'I bet she does. And she's used to sharing the outside toilet with a couple of other families as well as her own, so she's probably used to unpleasant smells. I'm sure you'll soon get used to things, love, and as you move up a scale you might get much nicer tasks to do. They're probably just throwing you in the deep end to see who is really serious and who isn't.'

Dianna nodded. 'Hopefully. A few of us are going out next Saturday night. First time we've been able to arrange anything out of the house. I'm looking forward to it. We're going to a coffee bar called the Rumblin' Tum on Hardman Street. It's not far from the Philharmonic Hall. Some of the older nurses say they have a good jukebox there and the atmosphere is friendly.' Dianna had also been told there were some nice lads that went in there – mainly art students and musicians – but she would keep that to herself for now. She didn't think her dad would approve of her dating boys just yet, and didn't want to put Bella in the position of keeping it from him.

Bella smiled. 'I'm sure you will have a good time. But just be careful, and don't you go wandering off from your friends. The city's not always the safest place at night for a young girl on her own.'

Dianna shrugged. 'Can't be any worse than New Orleans or New York, but I promise to watch my step. There are six of us going so we'll be fine in a gang, I'm sure. Safety in numbers, as they say.'

Dianna slicked her lips with glossy red lipstick and smiled at her reflection in the age-speckled mirror. She hadn't worn make-up for weeks as it wasn't allowed on the wards, and there'd been no point in bothering when she came off duty as most nights were spent lying on her bed studying. She smoothed down the full skirt of her red and white spotted cotton dress, one of Aunt Ruby's creations, and flicked her glossy ringlets back over her shoulders. Tonight she was off to the Rumblin' Tum coffee bar again, with the group of girls she'd become friendly with on the same course as her and Sally.

The first time they'd been, just before Christmas last year, she'd really enjoyed herself and had danced with a couple of local boys who told her they went to the art college. It was hard to get time off near the weekend, so she'd not been out as often as she'd have liked since then. But today was a Friday, and tomorrow she was going home to spend two days in a row with her family – a much-needed short break from ward work and studying. 'Come in,' she called as there was a knock on the door. She knew it was Sally.

'You ready?' Sally asked, swivelling her hips in her navy

blue figure-skimming dress. 'That red dress looks gorgeous on you; it matches your lippy perfectly! Can't wait for a dance. Hope them nice lads from the art college are in again tonight.'

Dianna smiled. 'Thank you. I'm glad Aunt Ruby chose this fabric; she'd read in a fashion article that spotty dresses are apparently becoming the latest thing. After such a long week, I can't wait to get on the dance floor and those boys did seem very nice. I'd like to get to know a bit more about them. It was so noisy and crowded last time we went; I couldn't hear a word anyone was saying. Mind you, we can't get too involved with a boy. Remember the warning? It's more than our lives are worth.'

They made their way to the reception area to meet up with the four friends they'd arranged to go out with. 'Ready, girls?' Dianna asked.

'As we'll ever be, Di,' replied Carol, a slim red-headed girl they'd met on their induction day and who was a born and bred Liverpudlian from the Aigburth area. 'If we hurry we'll be just in time for the ten past seven tram.'

As the tram they'd caught from outside the Royal stopped outside the Philharmonic Hall where they were to alight, the six excited friends grabbed their handbags and piled off the platform. They linked arms as they crossed the road and turned onto Hardman Street. An untidily dressed drunken man lurched across the road in their direction and called out to them.

''Ey, you lot, come over 'ere and give us a kiss and a fumble.'

'Sod off, you dirty old letch,' Carol shouted back at him, wrinkling her nose. 'Scruffy old bugger.' She shuddered. 'Bet he's not seen a bar of soap for at least a month. Reminds me of a horrible uncle of mine. He was always leering at me and my cousin and trying to touch us up. Eventually, the family had to completely disown him for being constantly drunk and disorderly.'

'Ah, get lost, yer all just cheap tarts, not worth the bother,' the man shouted, stumbling in front of a car, whose driver beeped its horn loudly. The drunk stuck two fingers up to the windscreen and lurched on his way.

Dianna remembered Molly's warnings about being out on her own in the city at night, and realised that she may have been too quick to dismiss them. She wouldn't like to meet someone like that drunken man when she wasn't surrounded by her friends. He reminded her of some of the creepy men her mom used to bring back to the apartment in New Orleans when she was a little girl. Dianna remembered how her own strong, tall dad had been beaten up by drunken thugs and left for dead after one of his first nights working at Bold Street studios, not long after they moved to Liverpool. Up until then she had never imagined that anyone would dream of picking a fight with her dad but, fuelled by hate and drink, the men had teamed up and the beating had been brutal. One of the thugs had been Fran's ex-husband and he and his cronies were now serving long prison sentences in Walton Gaol. She knew that Fran still felt guilty about what had happened, though of course no one blamed her for it. Prison was the best place for them, Dianna thought now as they stood outside the coffee bar, then shook the image out of her mind.

'Come on,' she said to Sally. 'Let's get inside where it's safer.' They strolled into the coffee bar and looked around at the striking black and white interior, the walls plastered with pages of old newspapers, varnished over to protect them. 'There's a table over there, near the jukebox.' Dianna pointed. 'Grab it quick before anyone else does.' She smiled, loving the decor; absolutely *everything* was black and white, including the tiled floor, which resembled a giant chessboard, the counter area and the Formica-topped tables and chairs, which reminded her of the diners back home in America. She shook off a little pang of homesickness that washed over her from nowhere.

Carol dashed across and sat down at the table, staking their claim. 'Right, what does everyone want to drink? Frothy coffee or Coca-Cola? Settle up with me later.'

'I'll come to the counter with you,' Dianna said, as the girls placed their orders with Carol. 'Help you to carry everything.'

As the young girl behind the counter loaded their assorted drinks onto a tray and Carol handed over a ten-shilling note and waited for her change, Dianna spotted the two boys they'd met a few weeks ago strolling in through the door. She felt her heart begin to beat a little faster. One blond and the other one, who had really caught her eye last time, dark, their hair styled in neat quiffs, both casually dressed in denim jeans and black jackets, they each had a guitar slung over their shoulders. She immediately thought of Levi and the guitar he'd proudly shown her last time she was home: his precious birthday present. He'd strummed a few chords and told her that he would soon learn to play some popular songs and she could sing them with him. When she was last home they'd sung a couple of African-American folk songs her dad had taught him the words to and his tutor had shown him the chords to, and she'd enjoyed doing it; seeing the pleasure on his face as she'd sung 'Go Tell it on the Mountain' to his accompaniment had been lovely. She was looking forward to seeing how he'd got on with his lessons in the last few weeks. She was sure that he'd have made a special effort to learn some songs for her visit tomorrow, and she looked forward to hearing what he had chosen.

The dark-haired boy looked across the room at the girls and even from that distance Dianna noticed how his brown eyes crinkled at the corners as he smiled. He waved a greeting and Dianna smiled back. Carol picked up the laden tray from the counter, thanked the young assistant, and carried it across to the table, Dianna following with a small jug of milk and a bowl of brown sugar cubes. She caught Sally's eye and nodded in the direction of the two boys, who were now standing by the jukebox talking to another couple of lads who'd just come in.

Sally's eyes opened wide. 'Is that the same pair from the other week?' she mouthed. 'The nice arty ones.'

Dianna nodded and sat down. 'The dark-haired one just smiled and waved at me,' she whispered. 'He's nice. Wonder if they are going to play something on their guitars?'

'Maybe, we'll have to see,' Sally replied.

'Shall we choose a record to play on the jukebox?' Carol suggested as the music stopped. 'It's gone a bit quiet. Do you want to have a look, Dianna, you're the nearest. Pick a couple of songs we all know?'

Dianna got to her feet and, trying not to stare at the boys with guitars, she studied the songs listed on the silent jukebox. She inserted a sixpence, pressed two buttons and hurried back to her seat as The Crew Cuts' 'Sh-Boom (Life Could Be a Dream)' broke the silence.

'Oh I love this,' Carol said, and started singing along. 'What else did you pick?'

'Wait and see,' Dianna teased, picking up her frothy coffee and taking a sip. 'Hmm, that's good for English-made coffee,' she said, licking the froth off her top lip. After the next song, Kitty Kallen's 'Little Things Mean a Lot', finished playing, Dianna felt a light tap on her shoulder and looked up to see the dark-haired boy standing behind her chair. She smiled shyly as he spoke.

'Good choice of songs,' he complimented her.

'Thank you.' She looked away from his direct gaze. His nice brown eyes twinkled as he looked at her.

'Err, mind if we sit at your table?' he asked, as his blond-haired friend joined him, dragging two chairs along behind him. 'I'm Stewart and this is Nigel.'

'Be our guests,' Sally said, batting her lashes in Nigel's direction. He smiled at her as she moved her chair over and

Dianna did the same to make room. 'I'm Sally, she's Dianna,' she told them.

'Nice to meet you, girls,' Stewart said.

'Don't mind us,' Carol said as the others laughed.

'All of you, in fact!' Stewart said, recovering quickly.

'Are you planning on playing those guitars tonight?' Dianna directed at Stewart. 'Or do you just carry them around for show?'

Nigel grinned. 'Sort of. No, we've just been for a music lesson,' he told her. 'We're not quite confident enough to play in public yet. One day soon, though, hopefully.'

Dianna smiled. 'My younger brother has just started having guitar lessons; he'll be playing me what he's learnt recently when I see him tomorrow. He's only eleven but he's doing quite well. Where do you go for your lessons?'

'Bold Street Enterprises,' Nigel replied. 'They've got a great tutor.'

Dianna nodded. 'They have indeed. My dad part-owns the studios. He's teaching my brother, in fact. It's nice that you go there.'

Stewart frowned. 'Your dad? Are you Earl Franklin's daughter then?'

'I am,' Dianna replied, rolling her eyes. 'For my sins.'

'Oh, your dad is a really nice guy. So, Levi Franklin is your brother? Does that mean you're *the* Dianna Franklin who he sang with when he won that talent show? The *Carroll Levis Discovery Show*? Oh wow. It's really good to meet you. We saw the certificate you were presented with on the studio wall in a frame. Your dad is really proud of you both. Always mentions you when we go in.'

Dianna nodded. 'That's me, I'm afraid.'

'Why afraid? You were great,' Nigel said. 'We listened to the show on the wireless. You both have fabulous voices. You can sing any songs you choose and do them justice.'

Dianna could feel her cheeks flushing, and looked across at Sally's raised eyebrows.

'I'm glad *you've* told her that,' Sally began. 'She *always* plays down her talent.'

'But why? You'll go a long way with that voice,' Nigel said.

Dianna shook her head. 'I don't want to sing any more, not professionally like that anyway. I'm training to be a nurse now, at the Royal; we all are,' she said, waving her hand around the table. 'And anyway, I'm a bit too old for Shirley Temple these days.'

Stewart laughed. 'There are loads of really good songs being written in America now. We get some of our records off the Cunard Yanks when they come into the docks with the big ships. They bring them over and sell them to us kids cheap. Big things are going to happen soon, according to the sailors.'

Dianna frowned. 'What sort of big things?'

Stewart shrugged. 'I don't really know, but that's what they say. There are kids with guitars all over the place, trying to do something different to what we all heard during the war years. Things are changing and me and Nige are getting ready for it by learning to play our guitars.'

Dianna smiled. They seemed very keen on the music side of life, so good luck to them.

'Do you fancy a dance?' Stewart asked. Someone had put another sixpence in the jukebox and Perry Como was singing 'Don't Let the Stars Get in Your Eyes'. He held his hand out to Dianna, who took it and got up to dance with him. She smiled as he looked down into her eyes. 'You're really pretty,' he said shyly. 'I don't suppose you'd fancy coming to the flicks with me one night, maybe tomorrow?'

Dianna chewed her lip and then nodded. 'I'd love to. I'll be at my dad's place tomorrow night, though,' she said. 'I've got two days off this weekend, so I'm going to catch up with my family. But I should be able to get out.'

'Okay, well where do they live? I'm over in Wavertree, but I could meet you down here if it's more convenient.'

'My family home is in Wavertree too, Queen's Drive,' Dianna said. 'I'll write you down the address. Maybe you could call for me there.'

Steward nodded. 'Yes, I can. We live just off Picton Road. We can go to the Abbey Picture House. They're showing *Doctor in the House* with Dirk Bogarde. And with you being a nurse, you never know, you might enjoy it.'

Dianna laughed. 'I probably will,' she said.

'And you can tell me all about how fabulous America is. I've always dreamed of going there one day.'

Dianna smiled. 'Okay, I will.' She looked across at Sally, who was just jumping to her feet to dance with Nigel. They seemed to be getting on well and hadn't stopped talking since they met. Dianna hoped things developed for the pair. It would be good to go out as a foursome sometime. As the song finished they all took their seats again and Stewart went over to the counter and brought back a tray of frothy coffees. The café was filling up with couples and there was little space to move around, let alone dance, but the atmosphere was lively. Someone chose Doris Day's 'Secret Love' on the jukebox and Stewart asked her to dance again. Dianna was conscious of the fact that time was moving on and they would need to dash for the last tram back to the Royal in less than half an hour, but she got to her feet and as they swayed together in the tiniest of spaces Stewart looked into her eyes and she was lost. She was so glad he'd already made another date with her and couldn't wait to see him again.

Earl made no effort to hide his disapproval when Dianna told him and Molly that she'd been invited to go to the pictures with

an art student to watch a film that night. He'd picked her and
Sally up earlier from outside the nurses' home and they'd
dropped Sally off at home on the way. Sally also had a date
tonight, with Nigel, but she wasn't sure where they were going
yet and she hadn't decided whether she was going to tell her
mam and dad about Nigel. She'd told Dianna she'd see how the
land lay and what sort of mood greeted her when she got home.

They'd just had a cuppa and a slice of cake that Molly had
made when Levi asked if he could play his guitar for Dianna.
She could tell he was itching to show her what he had learnt,
but that he'd been told to give her a moment to catch her breath.
Harry was running in and out of the dining room, treading mud
everywhere and wanting to show his big sister something he'd
been making in the garden. Baby Patti was upstairs in her cot,
having a mid-morning nap.

'So what do we know about this boy?' Earl asked, lighting a
cigarette and puffing hard on it.

Dianna shrugged. 'What do you want to know? He's from
Wavertree, he's an art student and his name is Stewart Jones.
Oh, and he's having guitar lessons at your studio with his friend
Nigel Brooks.'

'Ah.' Earl nodded, relaxing slightly. 'I know those two lads.
Stewart seems like a nice enough boy, well, they both do. Okay
then. At least he's coming here to pick you up, so Molly can give
him the once-over.' He smiled, seeming satisfied.

'Dad, don't you dare embarrass me when he gets here. It's
only a trip to the picture house. He's not asking you for my hand
in marriage. We're just friends, that's all.'

Molly cleared the mugs and plates from the table and poked
Earl on the shoulder. 'Leave her alone, you, and don't drag me
into it. Giving him the once-over indeed! As if I would. Dianna
doesn't get much of an opportunity to relax these days. It's nice
that she's been asked out by a decent lad. *And* she's going to see
Dirk Bogarde to boot. I wouldn't mind being taken out to the

pictures one night myself. Perhaps I could ask Mam to babysit and you can treat me?'

'Okay then, if that's what you'd like.' Earl looked suitably chastened. He smiled at Molly. 'I just need to make sure she's safe, that's all. She's my eldest princess, after all. You know what young lads are like these days. Maybe we should go with them, make it a double date,' he teased and laughed as Dianna looked horrified by his suggestion.

'Behave yourself.' Molly raised an ironical eyebrow in his direction and laughed. 'And yes, Earl, I think I do know what lads are like these days. No different to what they were like during the war years, I shouldn't wonder.'

'That's what bothers me.' Earl grinned and held his hands up in defeat. 'Okay, okay, I know when I'm beat. You just take care, that's all I'm saying,' he said to Dianna. 'Now you'd better go and listen to your brother. He's all set up and waiting to perform for you in the lounge.'

'I will, but first I have to check out what Harry is making outside. No doubt it will involve more mud, mess and worms.'

Dianna nodded in time to the tune Levi was playing on his guitar. He was note-perfect and she recognised the melody of The Stargazers' 'I See the Moon' with no problem. His look of concentration as he plucked the strings melted her heart. He was totally absorbed in what he was doing. She clapped as he finished and he smiled his gratitude.

'Will you sing it, Di?' he asked hopefully. 'Dad said you know all the words to this one.'

'Yeah, I do. Okay, why not, little brother,' she said, ruffling his curls affectionately. She nodded in time as he played the opening chords and then stood beside him and sang along, her voice pure and clear. She didn't notice her dad and Molly standing in the doorway until they clapped and cheered as the duo finished their song.

'Well done, the both of you,' Earl said, coming into the room. 'We're invited to Scotty's tomorrow afternoon for tea. Tammy and Ebony can't wait to catch up with you, Di. We'll have a sing-song while you're all together.'

Dianna smiled, knowing full well how her dad's mind was working. Get them all together, try to show her what she was missing. Well, he'd have to wait a bit longer while she concentrated on her career.

SEVENTEEN

Dianna's stomach flipped when Stewart took her hand as they walked down Queen's Drive towards the tram stop. Dad and Molly had been fine when he arrived and had welcomed him into their home. Dad had asked how his guitar lessons were going and if he was enjoying them.

'Very much, sir,' Stewart had replied politely.

Dad had thrown his head back and laughed, breaking the ice. 'You don't need to call me sir, son. Earl will do nicely.' He shook Stewart by the hand. 'Look after my girl, that's all I ask,' he'd finished as he saw them out.

Dianna had breathed a sigh of relief as the door closed behind them.

'I like your mum and dad,' Stewart said as they waited for the tram. 'I didn't realise she'd be white, and as Scouse as I am.'

'Oh, Molly's not my real mom,' Dianna said. 'She's my step-mother. My birth mom's family in America were originally from South Africa, many years ago, like Dad's family were.' She paused for a moment, wondering if she should continue, but Stewart seemed like an understanding boy. 'I'm afraid she wasn't a very good mom. She had problems and became an alcoholic. She neglected me. Dad got full custody of me after the war, before we emigrated here. But Molly is more like a real mom to me than my own ever was.'

Stewart squeezed her hand. 'I'm sorry you had a bad time when you were younger. So Molly is Levi's mum then?'

Dianna shook her head and, taking a deep breath, she explained the various branches of the mixed-up family she belonged to. 'I'm sorry if we seem to be a bit of a crazy muddle,' she apologised, sighing inwardly. It was enough to put any nice lad off, she thought. 'I'm afraid it's all down to my dad.'

'Hey, don't you be apologising for your family. They seem really nice and your dad seems to be well settled now.'

Dianna smiled. 'Oh, he is, thankfully. Molly is perfect for him. She keeps him in line. What about *your* family? How do they feel about you asking a Black girl out? That's if you've told them, of course.'

Stewart smiled. 'I have. They don't have a problem with it. Why would they? Oh, I know some awkward devils might do, but not my parents. Dad fought in the war with Americans alongside him, both Black and white, and he swears without the Yanks we'd never have won it. My mam also remembered listening to you and Levi singing on the wireless a while ago when you won the contest. She said you have a beautiful voice. She'd love to meet you when you next have time off.'

'Really?' Dianna smiled as the tram rumbled into view. 'I'd like that. It hasn't always been easy, you know, settling in Liverpool I mean, but as time goes on it seems to be more acceptable for white people to be friendly with Black people without certain others getting offended by it.'

'And that's how it should be,' Stewart said, as he helped her onto the tram platform. They found seats towards the rear of the carriage and he held on to her hand.

Dianna loved the way butterflies hurtled around in her tummy at his touch.

'By the way,' he said, 'Sally and Nige are meeting us outside the Abbey. Is that okay? You don't mind a double date?'

Dianna smiled. 'Not at all. That's great, Sal's been my best friend since the day I first started school here.'

'And Nige is mine, has been all my life.'

Sally waved to Dianna and Stewart as they jumped off the tram on Church Road North and made their way over to the Abbey Picture House building. The cinema was art deco in style, its name lit up with colourful neon lights. Inside the foyer, while she and Sally waited for Stewart and Nigel to buy the tickets, she stared up at the ceiling and the opposite wall, both covered in mirrors that reflected the twinkling lights. 'Nice, isn't it?' she said. 'Feels sort of magical; I've never been in here before.'

'I used to bring my younger brothers here to the matinees on Saturday afternoons while Mam got on with her housework,' Sally said. 'They loved it and actually stopped fighting for a couple of hours.'

Dianna smiled. Maybe she could bring young Harry one day, when he wasn't building mud houses for his worm collection. Stewart called them over to the sweet stand and asked them to pick their favourites.

'Let's have Payne's Poppets,' Sally said. 'I love them.'

Dianna nodded. 'Me too. I've not had them for ages.'

Two packets of Payne's Poppets in hand, the foursome were shown to their back-row seats by a hatchet-faced usherette who warned them they'd be chucked out if she saw any hanky-panky going on.

Sally laughed and took off her jacket. 'Miserable bugger,' she said. 'Bet she's going short of hanky-panky and it makes her feel jealous.'

'I'm not surprised,' Stewart said, helping Dianna off with her jacket. 'One glance from that one would soon sour the milk.'

'She has the same pained expression as one of our tutors,' Dianna observed, raising an eyebrow as the woman showed another young couple to their seats with the same brusque warning. 'Like she's sucking on a lemon.'

Stewart grinned. 'Or as my dad would say, she looks like a bulldog chewing a wasp!'

Dianna choked on a laugh and settled back in her seat as the lights went down and the newsreel began.

'You okay?' Stewart whispered as Dianna opened their packet of chocolate Poppets and offered him one.

She nodded. 'Yes, thank you, I'm fine. This is nice, just to be out and not working or studying.'

He smiled. 'Yep, it certainly is. Mind you, we're on college holidays until September. One more year and we'll be finished and looking for jobs.'

'Any idea what you'd like to do when you finish?'

He shook his head. 'Not really, err, well yes, I suppose I do, but it might not earn me any money and then Dad will say that two years at college was a waste of time.'

'You want to paint?' Dianna asked.

'More than anything,' he replied. 'And have my work on exhibition in a few galleries. Or do something with music. But earning a living with either will be hit and miss. I might have to be a draughtsman or something.'

'What about an architect?'

'Yep, or an architect. But I'd have to stay on longer at college.'

'My Uncle Scotty is an architect,' Dianna told him.

'Here, or in America?'

'Here. He came to Liverpool last year. He has his own consultancy now. I'll introduce you next time I'm home if you like and then you can ask him how you can get started, if it's what you choose to do.'

Stewart took her hand and squeezed it as the main feature

was advertised on the screen. The audience fell silent as the opening credits flashed up along with the film theme music. 'Thank you,' he said. 'That would be great.' He stopped as the light from the usherette's torch shone down the row and a 'be quiet down there' was uttered in his direction.

Dianna rolled her eyes, grinned at Stewart in the dim light and settled down to watching to see if life at St Swithin's Hospital was any better than life at the Royal, Liverpool.

'Earl, stop gawping out the window,' Molly said, walking into the lounge with two mugs of tea. 'You're worse than Net Curtain Nelly on Victory Street. She was always twitching the nets, noseying into everyone's business.'

'I'm not being nosy.' Earl sighed, tapping at his watch. 'The film would have finished over half an hour ago.'

Molly nodded and put the mugs on the coffee table. 'Yes, and it's Saturday night. It's their first date. They may have gone on to a coffee bar for a while. It's only half ten, stop fretting. The last tram isn't until half eleven. Come and sit down with me, for goodness' sake.'

As she spoke the garden gate clanged shut, Dianna let herself in at the front door and Earl breathed a deep sigh of relief. 'See, nothing to worry about,' she muttered.

'I'll remind you of that when Patti's a teenager,' he said, hurriedly sitting on the sofa beside her and picking up his mug. He smiled as Dianna popped her head around the door, a big smile on her face. 'Did you have a good time?'

'Yes thanks, Dad. The film was so funny. Nothing at all like real hospital life, well not the one I know, anyway. We just had a coffee with Sally and Nige before catching the tram.'

'Oh, I didn't realise they were going with you,' Earl said, relaxed now she was home.

'Neither did I until we were on our way. Stewart told me we were meeting them after we left here. It was so good to get away from our studying for a while.'

'Would you like a cuppa?' Molly asked, getting to her feet.

'I'll get it,' Dianna said. 'You stay there and rest for a while.' She took off her jacket, threw it over the back of a chair and headed towards the kitchen.

Molly smiled. 'See, all that worrying for nothing. You have to let her grow up and trust her own judgement. I know it's not easy, but Dianna is sensible. That's something to be thankful for.'

Earl stroked Molly's cheek gently. 'What would I do without your voice of reason, girl?'

Dianna, Tammy and Ebony hugged each other with delight. It was the first time the three had been together for a good few weeks. Levi tried to duck out of the way as Tammy threw her arms around him in the hallway and kissed him on the cheek. She laughed as he mumbled 'Yuck!', rubbed his face with his hand and went to find his dad and Uncle Scotty.

'Guess he's not too keen on being kissed,' Tammy said, grinning.

'He always does that,' Dianna told her, 'or ducks and runs when he sees Granny Mary coming towards him. He used to be cuddly and kissy, apparently.'

Molly appeared behind them, laughing. 'He's growing up fast. It's not a cool thing at his age, being kissed by an adult. If his mates found out they'd poke fun at him. Wait for a few more years and he'll be first in the queue when a pretty girl walks his way.'

They went to join the rest of the family in the dining room where a buffet tea was laid out on the table. Dianna was happy to spot a large slab of Aunt Ruby's famous ginger cake in the centre on a glass cake stand. Hopefully there'd be ice cream to have with it too. Aunts Ruby and Dolores greeted her and Uncle Scotty gave her a hug. As the family settled around the room on various sofas and chairs, with Patti safely ensconced in a high chair with a buttered crust to chew on, Scotty declared that he had some good news for them all. He waved a handful of thin blue paper covered in a spidery handwriting that Dianna recognised immediately as Grammy Franklin's. She held her breath as Uncle Scotty made his announcement, and tears sprang to her eyes as everyone cheered. Her uncle had booked a flight to England for Grammy and Grandpa Franklin so that they could spend Christmas and New Year with their family. And not only that, Uncle Levi, who her brother was named after, was coming with them to make sure they arrived safely – and, she suspected, because he wanted to check out Liverpool for himself.

'They'll all travel to New York first to spend a few days with Grammy's sister. BOAC have started to fly from New York to Manchester,' Scotty told them. 'So we'll need to drive up there and collect them, Earl. They arrive on the twenty-first of December, which is a Tuesday. They'll have a few days to rest before Christmas begins properly.'

'That's the best news,' Earl exclaimed. 'Mom didn't say anything about this in her last letter to me; I know she has been saving up but this trip will cost a fortune that she doesn't have.'

'Well, she wouldn't have said anything,' Scotty said with a grin. 'We wanted to surprise you all. I had some money left over from selling my house and I put it on one side to help with the cost of their trip. She agreed to keep quiet until we knew we had everything booked. She's so looking forward to meeting her new grandchildren and catching up with her three granddaughters.'

'I can't wait,' Dianna said excitedly. 'And Levi, you're gonna meet your namesake at last.' She smiled as her brother beamed.

'Now ain't that something special, son,' Earl said. 'Wait until you tell your mom and Bobby. What a wonderful celebration we are all going to have. Now what we need to plan is a very special Christmas show. I'll speak with Basil tomorrow, see if we can book the Empire Theatre for one night during their pantomime. You'll need to see if you can get that week off your course, Dianna. Tell them we have a special family time coming up. You're surely entitled to some holidays. You've only had the odd weekend free since you started. The sooner you ask them the better. Grammy and Grandpa are not getting any younger and may only be able to do this trip the one time.'

Dianna's heart sank. It was highly unlikely that she would get even a day off at that time of year. Last year she'd been given a few hours' leave on Christmas Day to have dinner with her family, but no other time at all between then and New Year. She would miss out on seeing Stewart at Christmas as well. He'd told her about the college parties that would be planned as soon as they were all back in after the holidays and how he'd like her to accompany him. All she could do was wait and see and if Sister Tutor said no she'd have to think again about how to wangle time off. Dad would want her to sing and rehearse for the new Christmas show; she'd seen the excited gleam in his brown eyes and no doubt he would be full steam ahead with planning in the next few weeks.

Molly patted her on the shoulder. 'Don't worry, Di. I'm sure we'll find a way around things.'

Dianna bit her lip and nodded. 'We will. Meanwhile, let's just enjoy this afternoon with everyone before Dad has to take me back later.' Stewart had promised to call her at the nurses' home tonight at nine o'clock, so she had that to look forward to as well.

EIGHTEEN

LIVERPOOL, DECEMBER 1954

Dianna groaned, forced her sleepy eyes open and rolled onto her side. She switched off the insistent alarm, sat up and shivered. The air in her room felt bitterly cold and the ancient pipes beneath the window were creaking and groaning as though getting ready to come to life and warm up. Pity the boiler wasn't stoked up with coke a bit earlier or even overnight, as anyone on an eight o'clock shift needed to be up at the crack of dawn to get showered, dressed and join the ever-lengthening queue for early breakfast. Dianna sighed and hugged her arms around herself as she remembered that in just one week's time Grammy and Grandpa Franklin and Uncle Scotty would be arriving in England.

When she'd asked for some time off during Christmas and New Year week, she'd been flatly refused. Her dad was fuming on her behalf and had threatened to come to the hospital and demand she be given at least one day off as it was a very special occasion. She'd begged him not to do that. She knew she'd get into trouble if he did, and tried pleading with the miserable Sister Tutor herself one more time, but to no avail. When she was informed again in no uncertain terms that she had to work, as it was the full-time trained staff who deserved the time off during the festive period over and above the junior cadets, she'd cried herself to sleep, that night and a few nights since. It wasn't so much the fact of her being told no, but rather the *way* she'd been told. Sister Tutor's ice-blue eyes and her taunting smirking mouth, as though she'd enjoyed seeing Dianna pleading for time off to see her grandparents, had made her almost walk away from the idea of becoming a nurse. Almost but not quite. As she'd left Sister Tutor's office she'd formed a loose plan of action in her mind, and no matter the consequences she was now sure she was going to go ahead with it. She'd feign illness two days before Christmas and insist she be allowed to go home to get well. If they refused again then she would walk out anyway. If push came to shove, they couldn't dismiss her for getting sick and not wanting to spread it about the ward.

Dianna was missing her family more and more as the days wore on. All the excitement of festively decorating the houses in readiness for the family visit, the rehearsals for the seasonal show her dad and Basil were busy organising. She'd had a few dates with Stewart as and when she was off duty and he called her each night on the nurses' home telephone, unless she was doing a late shift. He also sent her little letters in the post with sweet little drawings, and she treasured each one. Dianna was pretty sure she was falling in love with him. The way he looked at her told her he may feel the same. They had never yet been alone together and she was hoping that during the festive season they might get the chance. Perhaps at one of the parties. All that might be scuppered if she didn't have her plan ready. Other girls would vie for his attention if she wasn't with him, she was sure of it.

Dianna jumped out of bed, grabbed her dressing gown from the hook on the back of the door and dashed to the shower room, hoping against hope it was free. She bumped into Sally as she dashed back out again. 'See you in ten minutes,' she shouted after her friend. Back in her room she pinned her curls up – which was a job and a half these days as her hair had grown so long and unruly – and hurriedly pulled on her uniform. She'd just finished fixing her cap to her head as Sally hammered on the door. 'Coming,' Dianna called and hurried out to walk down the corridor to the big staff dining room.

'You okay, Di?' Sally asked, linking her arm. 'You look a bit weary, didn't you sleep well?'

Dianna shrugged. 'I did, but my dreams are a bit lively and I hate it when the alarm goes off and I have to leave them behind.'

Sally laughed. 'Lively, eh? And does Stewart feature in these dreams, by any chance?'

Dianna sighed. 'Occasionally. But it's mainly family stuff. I just feel very sad that I'm not able to spend a decent length of time with my grandparents when they arrive. I keep dreaming about times we spent Christmas together as a family when I was small. We always had such a lovely time. They're coming all that way and I'll be lucky to see them for half an hour after a shift.' She rolled her eyes heavenward. 'And have *you* looked at your shift patterns for that two weeks between now and New Year? Mine are absolutely awful. I'm sure they've been done on purpose. I'm on late shifts for nearly all of the time, or split shifts, which means I can't go anywhere in between as I'll never get any studying done for the February exams.'

Dianna and Sally queued for cereal, toast and mugs of steaming tea, then carried their trays to a table by the window.

'I've got a couple of odd days off,' Sally said as she placed her tray on the table and sat down. 'Mind you, I'm in for Christmas Day but I know I'll get a better dinner here than I would at home, so I'm not grumbling too much. The main thing I'm brassed off about is not seeing Nigel as often as I'd like. I'm even working late on Christmas Eve.'

'Me too.' Dianna nodded and took a sip of her tea. 'Stewart

said they're going to a few parties and now we won't be able to go with them. I hate that. I almost wish I'd never started this blooming training course in the first place now.'

Sally frowned as she spread marmalade on her toast. 'But you like it, normally, don't you?'

Dianna shrugged her shoulders and lowered her voice. 'I did at first, but I've not been happy for some time that I seem to be given all the horrible, messy jobs. I'm paired with Alice Haynes, as you know, and she just gets the nice work. I don't feel that I'm learning anything useful at all, apart from how to clean the sluice and empty bedpans. I'm sick of it, to be honest.'

'Alice Haynes is always Sister's pet,' Sally said, turning to look at the girl in question, who was sitting at a table a few feet away. All the cadets worked in pairs and Sally would have loved to be paired with Dianna but it wasn't to be. 'And you know *why* that happens, don't you?'

Dianna shook her head, frowning. 'No I don't, what do you mean?'

'They try and keep it quiet, but she's Sister Tutor's cousin's only daughter. Her family are quite well-to-do, live in Woolton and that Alice thinks she's better and above anyone else.'

Dianna gasped. 'I didn't know they were related. Well, she's definitely kept that quiet. So it's down to favouritism; well, that's not right, is it? And anyway, half of my family *also* live in Woolton. My brother Levi lives there with his parents for starters. Two can play at that game then.' She fell silent as Alice Haynes' over-loud voice told her breakfast companion that she was spending Christmas with her family and was 'soooo' looking forward to it.

Dianna's stomach tightened as she listened to the girl crowing about getting as much time off as she'd requested, including Christmas Eve and Christmas Day. She knew Alice saw her grandparents a lot, as she'd mentioned them once or twice in the odd conversation they'd had. They kept a horse that Alice rode regularly.

'You are so lucky to get a break,' the other girl at Alice's table gushed. 'I've got one day off in between Christmas and New Year and that's it.'

Well, it was one more day than Dianna had got, she thought angrily as she watched the two girls rise to their feet and walk out of the dining room. And they were both girls who had local families they could see at any time. She nibbled at her toast and then dropped it back onto her plate, her appetite gone. It really wasn't fair. She felt certain that Sister Tutor had done this on purpose. Dianna didn't expect any favours – she just got on with the jobs she was given without complaint, even when they made her gag – but this was different. She felt as though she'd been unfairly singled out and she wondered why. Sister Tutor had never really been that nice to Dianna, and she was also unkind to other cadets who grumbled about the tasks they were given to do. It dawned on Dianna that she seemed to favour the girls from better-off families; not that Dianna's family were poor, but there was something the tutor didn't seem to like about her. Then as she looked around it struck her, a thought that had never really crossed her mind until today. She was the only Black cadet on this course. There were a couple of other Black girls on the state registered nursing course, but they were a good few years older and had probably had a different tutor as cadets. There was no doubt about it; she was the only young Black nurse in the hospital. Her aunts were of course Black too, but they had done their training in America and not here, and were senior staff and well respected in their fields of theatre and maternity. She'd never heard them complaining about anything unfair.

'What's up?' Sally said. 'You've gone all quiet on me.'

'I've just had a thought,' Dianna said, pushing her uneaten

breakfast to one side. 'I'm the only Black girl here on this course. Is that why she doesn't like me? Is it because of my skin colour? Sister Tutor, I mean.'

Sally looked shocked. 'No, Dianna, surely not? She's just a nasty cow and her cousin's daughter is tarred with the same brush, it would seem.'

But Dianna shook her head. 'It's because I'm Black, I'm convinced of it. She's probably had a word with all the ward sisters and told them to give me all the shitty jobs and to give Alice the nice ones. That's happening all the time and it's been on *every* ward so far. There has to be a reason for it. It's because she reckons that's all I'm fit for.' She got to her feet, scraping back her chair with force, attracting the attention of the rest of the diners.

'Dianna, sit back down, everyone is staring at you,' Sally pleaded, grabbing hold of Dianna's hand. 'Don't do anything rash, please.'

But Dianna wasn't listening. Her voice rising, she continued, 'I'm going to her office and having it out with her. How dare she treat me like this? It's insulting. I thought the days of slavery were long over, but she seems to think I'm fit for nothing but cleaning up other people's mess. I was under the impression I was here to learn nursing, not to be a skivvy. I could have left school without my O levels and been a cleaner if I'd chosen to. I've worked hard for nothing.' With tears running down her cheeks, Dianna fled out of the dining room with Sally hot on her heels, calling for her to slow down.

She stopped dead halfway down the corridor and Sally ran into the back of her. Dianna whipped around. 'You stay here, Sally. I have to do this on my own. I don't want you getting into any trouble because of me.' Adrenaline coursing through her veins, Dianna rushed back to her room, leaving Sally staring after her. Grabbing her navy blue cape and draping it around her shoulders, she left the nurses' home and hurried across the hospital grounds to the Preliminary Training School building. She pushed the door open with such force so that it hit the wall inside with a loud bang, then dashed through and hurried down the narrow passageway to Sister Tutor's room. She hammered on the door and, ignoring the murmuring of voices she could hear from inside, she barged in, unannounced and without waiting to be invited. Sister Tutor and Matron were sitting at the desk with a sheaf of papers spread out in front of them. Dianna cringed inwardly, but she wasn't backing down now. The two women gaped silently at her. Both had the same ice-blue eyes. Angry red spots appeared high on Sister Tutor's cheeks.

She spoke first. 'Nurse Franklin, how dare you barge into my office uninvited?' She spluttered on her words, spittle flying across the desk. 'Your behaviour is insolent and totally uncalled for.' She got to her feet and leant both hands on her desk, almost snorting down her thin nose, on which was precariously balanced a pair of wire-framed spectacles.

Matron took a deep wheezing breath and stared at Dianna, her thin lips pursed but silent. Her cutting gaze spoke volumes, although her eyes were not quite as cold as Sister Tutor's. Both women exchanged looks and shook their heads.

'Well, I'm waiting, girl,' Sister Tutor barked, her tone icy.

Dianna stared coldly back. From somewhere deep within her she found the courage and realised she wasn't as scared of confronting these two women as she thought she'd be. She took a deep breath, trying to calm her nerves as she didn't want to burst into tears just yet. 'I'm here,' she began, speaking quietly but determinedly, 'because I feel that I am being treated unfairly by various members of your staff, due to the colour of my skin.' She swallowed hard as the women looked at one another again. 'And I would like to report this matter right away.'

Matron frowned and shook her head. 'Nurse Franklin, I

hope you realise that is a very serious accusation to make. What proof do you have of such claims?'

'Plenty,' Dianna said and before she could lose her nerve she told Matron of all her grievances, dating back to her first weeks on the wards and finishing with her request for time off to see her grandparents at Christmas being refused. As she finished she burst into noisy tears and Matron came around to her side of the desk and sat her down on a chair.

'Now calm down, Nurse Franklin, and take a few deep breaths. Sister Tutor, would you kindly get her a glass of water please.' The latter was directed coldly to the other woman.

Sister Tutor tutted loudly but half-filled a glass at the small sink in the corner of the room.

Dianna took the half-full glass that was thrust in her direction and took a sip. 'Thank you,' she said, directing her thanks at Sister Tutor, who stared at her as though she was something nasty on the sole of her shoe. Her pinched and angry face was more than Dianna could bear to look at and instead she turned her gaze to Matron, who at least looked a bit more kindly, if not startled by Dianna's revelations about Sister Tutor's niece, favouritism, and the serious accusations of racial prejudice.

Matron half-smiled and nodded and Dianna felt herself relaxing a little. 'I don't think I want to do this any more,' she said quietly. 'Be a nurse, I mean. If I can't feel comfortable here and certain that I'm being treated equally then I don't want to finish my training.'

Matron sighed and nodded slowly. 'That is your decision to make, Nurse Franklin, of course. You have the makings of a very good nurse, but I quite understand *why* you feel you have been treated unfairly and I will look into this immediately. I *do* take uncalled-for prejudices against a person of a different colour very seriously and will deal with the matter accordingly. However, I think a good break at home with your family will be very beneficial for you at this time, certainly until after Christmas. I will telephone your father to come and collect you this morning. Meanwhile, if you would like to go and pack everything you feel you will need for the next couple of weeks and then wait in your room until Home Sister comes to let you know your father is here. And Nurse Franklin, may I ask that you do not discuss this matter with any other members of staff for the time being. Thank you.'

Dianna got to her feet and put down the glass of water on the desk. If looks could kill then Dianna knew she would drop down dead now on the spot from the look Sister Tutor shot her. The woman obviously knew she was in for an interrogation with regards to her family member and Dianna's accusations. If only she'd been paired with any other nurse than Alice Haynes this might not have happened. Just her luck. 'Thank you,' she directed at Matron, who indicated with a nod that she could leave the room. Sister Tutor looked away and Dianna was gratified to see an embarrassed expression on her thin face.

She hurried back to her room and packed her suitcase. She stripped off her uniform, left it folded on the bed, and got dressed in some of her own clothes. She tore a page from her notebook and wrote a quick letter to Sally, who would already be on duty by now, telling her she was going home for a couple of weeks and would phone her, or for Sally to phone her dad's house when she had time. She would tell her what was happening, no matter what Matron had requested she do. Sally could be trusted to keep things quiet. She pushed the note under Sally's door and went back into her room to wait for her dad to come and collect her. Dianna already knew in her heart of hearts that she wouldn't be coming back to this room ever again. No matter what the outcome of Matron and Sister Tutor's discussion, her mind was already made up. She'd miss her best friend dearly, but she was not going to finish her cadet nurse training now under any circumstances. She'd already suffered prejudice in America, then here at school from those horrible lads, and now at the hospital in her chosen career. She would not be beaten, though, and was determined that one day all people would treat her with respect – and hopefully look up to her – no matter what colour her skin was.

'Come on, one more time, girls,' Bobby cajoled from his position behind the piano in the Bold Street studios. 'Then I'll let you have an hour off to go and wander around the city, as long as you bring cakes back for us poor overworked men.'

Dianna laughed. She, Tammy and Ebony were down at the studios rehearsing for next week's show at the Empire Theatre. The show was scheduled for Wednesday the 29th, tucked in between Christmas and New Year week; billed once more as the Franklins, they were to sing four songs, the final one being Irving Berlin's 'White Christmas', which was a current big hit for Bing Crosby. That was the song Bobby wanted a repeat of right now. Dianna felt happier than she'd felt for some time. She missed her friends at the hospital and the nice bits of nursing, but definitely not the more mundane tasks she'd been bogged down with. Grammy and Grandpa Franklin had arrived two days previously and they were taking it easy at Scotty's house while they recovered from the tiredness that came with the time difference. It had been so good to see them, and as soon as Grammy had held her in her arms Dianna knew that nothing

else on earth mattered more than that precious moment, the one
that cruel Sister Tutor had tried to deprive her of.

Sally had told Dianna that an urgent inquiry had been
conducted right away at the hospital and Sister Tutor had been
advised to resign from her position immediately. If she refused
she would be removed from her job for encouraging racial
inequality among the staff. She had vanished with immediate
effect and much to Dianna's amusement, Alice Haynes, her
cousin's daughter, had had all her Christmas holiday leave
cancelled, as there was no one else to cover for Dianna's shifts.
After discussing things with her dad and Molly and feeling
absolutely certain that she didn't want to continue her training,
Dianna had written to Matron and informed her that she
wouldn't be coming back to finish her course. A letter had
arrived back by return of post with an apology from Matron and
the hospital management, with an assurance that should she
change her mind she would be welcomed back, but that in the
meantime they wished her the best of luck in whatever new
career she chose.

Dianna was enjoying helping out at the studio and of course
they were all so busy now with the upcoming show rehearsals.
She had confided in Granny Mary that she would miss the
caring side of nursing a bit, but that was all. Yesterday Basil had
had a quiet word with her after Mary had spoken to him about
an idea she'd had. He'd asked her if, after Christmas, when
things had quietened down at the studio and her grandparents
had returned to the USA, she would like a little job helping out
with caring for Fenella, who was now totally housebound unless
someone took her out in her wheelchair. Dianna liked Aunty
Fen, as she called her, and said she would love to do that. She'd
be looking after her for a couple of afternoons a week and would
help her to get ready and take her to her WI meetings at nearby
St Peter's Church Hall, as well as visits to the library and out for

tea occasionally. Fenella had been the president in charge of the Wavertree WI for many years, but since moving to Woolton and becoming more and more incapacitated she'd had to give up her position, and instead had joined her local branch as a member for when she could manage to get to meetings. Dianna felt sure they would get along just fine. It was something they would both benefit from. She loved helping Molly with the little ones as well. She certainly had enough things to do to keep her busy, and of course Stewart was delighted that she could now accompany him to some of the parties he'd been invited to over the festive season. With the small wages her dad paid her for helping at the studios, and the money Basil had promised her for helping to look after Fenella, Dianna could still feel independent.

Tammy and Ebony only had until next July before they finished school and then they were both determined they wanted to either sing or work at the studios, if they could get the bookings that is. With the three girls now where he wanted them, Earl had big plans for the trio as well as for Levi, who haunted the studios with his presence as soon as he left school each day and had done the same throughout the holidays so far. Fran and Bobby had been busy writing new songs for the Bryant Sisters and Earl had asked them to think about writing some suitable songs for the teenagers. All in all, Dianna's world was a happy place to be in right now.

Fran took her warm jacket down from the coat rack in the hall and pulled a woollen knitted bobble hat over her freshly washed and dried hair. She tossed a matching light blue scarf around her neck and dug in her pockets for her mittens. Her mam had been busy and Fran and Lorraine were well kitted out for the winter weather. It was a cold morning and she wanted to dash to the shops for something for tea before she went into Edie's house next door for a cuppa. Bella was coming down later for a catch-up. Their kids were all with various grandparents as the three of them planned to go into the city for a bit of last-minute present shopping before heading into the studios for the Christmas show rehearsal. Life was busier now than it had been for some time. She really missed having Earl's family living next door and now that Ruby had gone to live with Scotty, the house was empty and eerily quiet. But still, better that than having somebody horrible living next to her.

As she let herself out of the front door Fran was aware of the dirty nets across the street twitching. Nosy cow, she thought as she hurried up Victory Street, grinning to herself. No doubt her movements were being noted down and would be conveyed to Frankie at some point. Well, there was little he could do about it, so she wasn't going to worry her head too much. She had had a few more scribbled notes shoved through her letter box, but she'd torn them up unread and pushed the bits of paper through the nosy woman's letter box.

With a bit of luck, and if all went according to plan, she'd soon be giving them something else to gawp at. Last week Fran had accepted a date with Sam Stevens, a young drummer with one of the bands that used the upstairs studio rehearsal area. Sam was a nice man, a couple of years Fran's junior but they always got on really well whenever they had met. She was looking forward to getting to know him better and he had invited her to the Grafton Ballrooms for the Christmas Eve dance. He was playing with the resident band but had told her the other band members' wives and girls would be there so she wouldn't be alone when he was on stage. Lorraine was staying at her mam's overnight and Fran was being picked up from Victory Street by Sam, who would then drop her off at her mam's when the dance was over, to stay there for Christmas. It would all work out perfectly and that nosy cow would see her going out all dolled up for the night and then not coming home. See what she made of that, Fran thought, grinning broadly as she joined the queue in the greengrocer's.

∾

'So are all the kiddies invited as well?' Edie asked, as she handed out steaming mugs of tea to Bella and Fran. Bella had just told them that everyone was invited to Scotty's house for late tea on Christmas Day.

'Yep, every one of them,' Bella said. 'They're doing it a bit later so that the older family members can have a nap after the queen's speech. Then they won't be falling asleep too early. Scotty has asked if we'll sing, and Dianna, the girls and Levi will do a few songs as well. It should be a lovely night and we can all have a rest on Boxing Day.'

'We'll need it,' Fran said. 'I'll be having a late one on Christmas Eve as well.'

'Are you looking forward to your date with Sam?' Bella asked, reaching for a mince pie that was fresh out of Edie's oven.

'Do you know, I really am,' Fran said. 'I'm actually beginning to finally feel free of Frankie now. Oh I know he still thinks I'm his, but he's banged up for donkey's years now, so he can't get to me. And I'm not afraid of that stupid woman opposite me and her husband either. I think they've got the message since I posted those daft bits of paper back through her letter box. Same old threats as the one I flew back at her. Once our Don and Phil had a word with them they seem to have backed off. Although she still twitches the nets when I go out.'

Edie smiled and patted Fran's hand. 'Good. It's time for you to move on. Sam seems like a really nice man and he definitely fancies you. You only have to see the way his face lights up when you come into the studio control room.'

'Do you really think so?' Fran chewed her lip. 'I guess Frankie took a lot of my confidence on that score, but it's slowly coming back, bit by bit. Maybe Sam will help to speed things up. Oh God, now I sound like an old car that needs fixing.' She laughed and Bella and Edie joined in.

'It's good to see you getting back to your old self,' Bella said. 'We've got the show to look forward to next week as well. Dust off the old uniforms ready for a bit of Andrews Sisters stuff. And Di and her cousins are so excited.'

'Is Dianna really okay?' Fran asked. 'I know she seems to be enjoying singing again, but giving up the nursing course was a big decision for her to make.'

Bella nodded. 'She seems to be fine. The old witch has left the hospital with no argument and that leads me to believe Dianna didn't imagine the discrimination. I think that tutor just had it in for her from day one. I hope Levi doesn't encounter anything like that when he's ready to start working. Although if it's up to Earl and Bobby, he'll be on stage for most of his teens, or at least doing some sort of work with the recording studio.'

'Good business to be in with all the new records the Cunard Yanks are bringing over from America,' Fran said. 'I think we're in for some exciting times in the music world over the next few years. If he can get to grips with writing his own songs, he'll do well.'

～

Dianna smoothed down the skirt of her jade-green silk dress that Aunt Ruby had made for her. The colour looked lovely against her skin and she had a band of the same silk fabric tied around her hair. Aunt Ruby had worked her magic and trimmed and tamed her curls back into the glossy ringlets that

Dianna loved. The harsh water at the nurses' home and lack of coconut shampoo when she'd run out had played havoc with her locks over the last few months, so it was good to have it pampered back to life again. She shook her head and her curls bounced on her shoulders. Dad and Molly had bought her a new wool coat for Christmas and had given it to her earlier so that she would look smart going out tonight. The coat was a lovely shade of red with a big collar and lapels, turn-back cuffs and a wide tie belt in the same fabric to nip her narrow waist in even further. She slipped her feet into black patent-heeled shoes and picked up her matching handbag from the bedside table. She smiled at her reflection in the full-length mirror on the inside of her wardrobe door, loving the way her lippy matched the red of her coat.

'Wow, you look stunning,' her dad said, and Molly nodded her agreement. Dianna smiled and went downstairs to wait in the lounge for Stewart to call for her. Tonight she would meet some of his art school friends for the first time. They were going to a party being thrown by one of them at his family home in Woolton. Despite looking forward to the evening, Dianna felt nervous and wished Sally was able to join them with Nigel tonight, but sadly she was working and Stewart had told her that Nigel was doing something with his family.

'Thanks, Dad, Molly,' she said, jumping as the doorbell rang. 'That'll be Stewart,' she began as she heard Levi thunder downstairs, open the door and greet her boyfriend. Damn, if those two got talking guitars they'd never get out tonight. Mind you, it was nice they got on so well and had a shared passion. She smiled as Levi led Stewart through to the lounge.

She was gratified to see Stewart's face showing his pleasure as he took in her appearance. 'You look gorgeous,' he said quietly, 'you really do.'

'Yeah,' Levi said, grinning cheekily. 'You remind me of a Christmas tree, sis, all green and red.'

Molly pretended to clip him around the ear, stifling a giggle. 'Behave yourself. And go and get your jacket and shoes on so your dad can run you back to your ever-suffering parents. Hey, and you'd better be good because Father Christmas doesn't visit naughty boys, so you've not got long to redeem yourself.'

'I'm not falling for that one at my age,' Levi said as he ducked out of her reach, his brown eyes twinkling, before Aunty Molly could really clip his ear. 'And my mam says I'm the apple of her eye, so there,' he finished as they all burst out laughing.

'It's a madhouse. Shall we go?' Dianna said to Stewart.

He grinned. 'Of course, seeing as you're ready.'

'Have a lovely time!' Molly said, following them to the door, Earl on her heels.

'Take care of my princess,' Earl called after them. 'And don't have her home too late.'

'I won't,' Stuart called back. 'Will midnight be okay, seeing as it's a special night?'

Earl nodded. 'Yes, but no later.'

Dianna rolled her eyes as Stewart took her hand and they hurried along to the tram stop. 'Sorry about that,' she said. 'Levi's just showing off to try and impress you.'

'Ah, it's all right. I wish I had a brother, or even a sister,' he said. 'It's lonely at times, being an only child.'

'I know,' Dianna agreed. 'I was one for ten years until we came here. Now I'm one of four.'

As they stood at the tram stop the queue grew longer and people, all dressed up for a good night out, called out season's greetings to one another. Stewart looked into her eyes and her stomach flipped as he smiled. 'Have you got any family stuff planned for Boxing Day?' he asked.

She shook her head. 'Not at the moment. Tomorrow is our big extended family party at my Uncle Scotty's place, but no one has said anything about Boxing Day yet.'

He nodded. 'My mam told me to ask you to tea if you can make it. My parents would love to meet you. They've got tickets for the show at the Empire next week.'

Dianna smiled. 'Have they? Really? I would love to meet them and have tea with you. Why don't you come to Uncle Scotty's with me tomorrow afternoon? Then you can meet the rest of my family, especially my Grammy and Grandpa Franklin. It's a special time and we might not be able to all get together again for ages.'

'Will it be okay?' Stewart asked anxiously. 'I mean, should you ask your parents first maybe?'

'I'm sure it will be fine,' Dianna replied. 'But if it makes you feel better we can maybe get back home a little earlier tonight. I know my dad will still be up playing Santa and filling the kids' stockings. I can ask him but I know he'll say yes.'

'Okay then, we'll do that,' Stewart said as the tram rumbled into view. 'Here we go.'

Dianna looked up at the large double-fronted house that Stewart's art school pal lived in. A beautifully decorated Christmas tree twinkled in the large bay window to the right of the front porch. The curtains were drawn back on the left-side bay window and she could see people milling around, silhouetted by the lamplight inside. It looked lovely and cosy and she shivered as they waited on the doorstep for someone to answer their knock. The door was flung open and revealed a girl in a blue party dress that matched the colour of her eyes. Her blonde hair was glamorously styled into waves, reaching down past her shoulders. She invited them inside. 'I'm Carol,' she said, 'Vic's sister. Come on in. Victor!' she bellowed over her shoulder. 'Some more of your friends are here.'

'Come on, Caz,' a tall and skinny dark-haired lad shouted

from the doorway of the dining room. 'We can dance to this one.'

'Coming, George,' she called over the loud jazz that was playing in the room. 'Gotta go,' she said to Dianna and Stewart. 'Here's our Vic now, he'll look after you.' She dashed away as her brother, the image of his blue-eyed sister, hurried into the hall and greeted Stewart, who introduced him to Dianna.

'Ah. The lovely Dianna,' he began, taking her hand. 'I've heard so much about you. Been dying to meet you. And you are just as beautiful, if not more so, than Stewart said you were. You're, well, you're just so American.'

Dianna exploded with laughter, liking this slightly crazy friend of her boyfriend's. 'I'll take it as a compliment.'

'Oh you must,' he said, 'because that's exactly what it was meant to be. Now come along and meet everyone else and get a few drinks down you. There's plenty of choice and glasses in the kitchen on the big table.'

Stewart helped Dianna out of her coat and hung both his and hers on a rack in the hall, and Victor led them both through into the kitchen, where they were warmly greeted by his many friends.

As the night wore on Dianna was so glad she'd made the decision to give up nursing. To think she would have missed tonight if she hadn't. There were quite a lot of single girls around, hungrily eyeing up her boyfriend, but thankfully he was unaware and only seemed to have eyes for her. Quite a few people asked her about her singing career and where she planned on taking it. A few had got tickets for the show next week, which made her feel a bit nervous, but she hoped that when she answered their questions she sounded as though she knew what she was talking about.

'Shall we get a bite to eat?' Stewart asked halfway through the night. 'It'll help to soak up a bit of the alcohol from that punch we've been knocking back. God knows what's in it but it's so flipping strong.'

Dianna nodded. Food was a good idea. She felt a bit tipsy and light-headed. It wouldn't do to go home drunk. Her dad would go mad. She'd only ever been allowed a drop of sherry on special occasions and wasn't used to alcohol on a regular basis. They made their way into the dining room, where a buffet was laid out on a large table. The volume was turned up loud and music blasted out from a highly polished wooden radiogram in one of the alcoves beside a large marble fireplace. It looked expensive. Good job Vic's parents were out as they would no doubt go mad at their pride and joy being hammered so loudly, Dianna thought. She knew her dad would be; he treated their own radiogram with the utmost respect and expected everyone else in the family to do the same when they played their records. Several couples were dancing and others were draped over the sofas and chairs locked in one another's arms, sharing cuddles and passionate kisses. Dianna looked away, feeling embarrassed. One couple close by were hardly coming up for air. Surely they could find a more private part of the house to carry on with their canoodling?

'Ah, listen,' Stewart said as he filled a plate with sandwiches and a couple of sausage rolls for him and Dianna to share. The opening chords to a new song that had just been released and had shot up the music charts last week to number four began to play. 'Shake, Rattle and Roll' was unlike anything Dianna had ever heard. Sung by an American called Bill Haley with his backing band the Comets, it was so different and filled her with a feeling of excitement like no other song had ever done before. She'd recently seen a picture of Bill Haley, a plumpish man in a checked draped-style jacket with an elaborate kiss-curl decorating his forehead.

'They call it rock and roll, you know,' Stewart told her, sitting down on the sofa and patting the adjacent seat for her to join him. 'The Cunard Yanks say it's the next big thing in America and it's coming to England very soon, and they should know. They were selling copies of this record down the docks last week to the kids who were after new records. When me and Nige went down after college finished they had none left. No doubt Vic grabbed a copy while he could. I've read about a film being made that's supposed to be out next month called *Rock Around the Clock* and Bill Haley and the Comets sing and act in it. We just have to go and see it, Di.'

She helped herself to a sandwich and nodded. 'We will. I like this sort of sound. It's got more life than some of the stuff Dad wants us to sing. I don't want him to turn us into another Bryant Sisters type of act. Some of their wartime songs are too old-fashioned for us. He's asked Bobby and Fran to write us some new stuff. They need to hear this, though, and try and bring us up to date.'

Steward nodded. 'Me and Nige fancy forming a duo and having a bash at writing our own songs eventually. We feel more confident with the guitars now, so it's time to think about doing something with them. Maybe you could sing with us occasionally.'

Dianna swallowed hard on the sandwich she was just finishing. 'Sing with you?'

He nodded. 'Yeah, don't you think that would be a nice thing to do?'

She smiled. 'I guess it would be nice. I'll have to see what Dad says, though. He has plans to manage my cousins and me, but singing with you would be something a bit different to do. And the twins are still at school until July so we can't perform professionally for a while – apart from singing in the family shows, of course. We'll ask him and see what he says.' She put the empty plate down on a nearby coffee table and sank back against the soft cushions on the comfortable sofa. Stewart took her into his arms and kissed her. Dianna snuggled closer to him and lost herself in his embrace. One day soon they'd hopefully get the chance to be alone, but that wasn't going to happen tonight. Perhaps just as well, she thought now, as she still felt a bit squiffy, as Molly would say, and when they eventually did get the opportunity to be alone she wanted to be perfectly sober and to remember every minute of the time for the rest of her life.

TWENTY

As she stood in the wings with her cousins, watching her dad performing Johnnie Ray's 'Such a Night' to a packed theatre, Dianna was filled with pride. He could still sing well and he had something about him, a spark of charisma. He moved effortlessly around the stage and his voice was so much richer than Johnnie Ray's, in Dianna's opinion. She smiled as he took a final bow to cheers and loud clapping. She hoped Stewart and Nigel were here in their complimentary front-row circle seats they'd been given by Earl and that Stewart's parents were enjoying the show so far. Her first meeting with his parents on Boxing Day had gone so well and she'd been made to feel very welcome in their home. And Stewart had been warmly welcomed by her own family on Christmas Day. Grammy had immediately laid claim to him and he'd sat beside her for most of the evening, loving her tales of back home and the music scene in New Orleans. She'd told him about the gospel singing her children had all started with and how Earl had shown promise and had expanded on his talents with the American air force band he'd joined. All in all, Christmas had been a great success and it made Dianna feel sick to the stomach when she thought of how she may well have missed it all if she hadn't realised what was going on at the hospital. She shook the horrible thoughts away and turned her attention back to her dad.

'And now,' Earl began as the cheers and clapping faded. 'We have a real treat in store for you all. A trio of three young ladies who are originally from America but who now all reside here in your fabulous city of Liverpool. I give you my dear daughter Dianna and my nieces, Tammy and Ebony, known collectively as the Franklin Girls.'

The three of them ran on stage and Dianna smiled when she realised the loudest whistles were coming from her boyfriend and her uncles and grandpa. Dressed in her red velvet Christmas dress made by her kind Aunt Ruby and the twins' mom, she felt every part the star and her confidence soared as the band played the opening to Rosemary Clooney's 'This Ole House'. Their harmonies on the Chordettes' 'Mr Sandman' sounded perfect to her ears and Dianna took lead vocals on Jo Stafford's 'You Belong to Me'. They finished their spot with Bing Crosby's 'White Christmas' and took bows to tumultuous applause and cheers. Dianna felt a tear running down her cheeks as her dad praised the three of them. He was so proud; it showed on his face. She had done the right thing, she was more certain of that now than she'd ever been. They ran offstage. Levi was up next with his guitar. He played a couple of solo songs, including 'The Whole World in His Hands'. He had everyone singing along with him and clapping. Peeking out from her place backstage, Dianna could see the front row of the circle and her grammy's proud smile as she clapped along to her grandson's song. What a wonderful time this was for her. To see her African-American musical heritage carried across the Atlantic over generations, and to see so many members of her family performing in one show. What wonderful memories she would take back home with her. Stewart had told Dianna that Grammy had invited him to visit anytime he wanted to and be sure to bring Dianna along with him. She smiled as she recalled his excitement. He'd certainly been a hit with Grammy.

The Bryant Sisters finished the show with their Andrews Sisters spot, which had the audience joining in, and Bella's solo of 'We'll Meet Again' had the tears flowing as it always did. Dianna bet that many members of tonight's audience were reliving their time during the war years and thanking God they had somehow survived it and were here tonight as proof that Liverpool still stood proud in spite of all the destruction.

As she came offstage Fran smiled at Sam, who was the show's drummer tonight with the studio band. He winked and mouthed 'See you later' as the curtains closed and the theatre lights went on.

'Well, that was wonderful,' she said as the Bryant Sisters hurried to get changed out of their military uniforms. 'What a fabulous audience.'

'Weren't they just,' Bella agreed. 'It was so good to have our menfolk in the band as well.' Bobby had played piano tonight and Fran's husband Stevie had played saxophone. They all looked as though they'd enjoyed themselves just as much as the girls had.

Basil was waiting in the corridor for everyone as they came out of the dressing rooms. 'Well done, each and every one of you. I'm so proud. That was as good a show as any of the ENSA shows we put on during war time. Now, there's a buffet waiting to be eaten in the green room, if you'd all like to make your way there. The family are waiting for you. Your Stewart and his mate are there too, and his parents,' he directed at Dianna.

Fran sought out Sam, who took her in his arms and dropped a kiss on her lips. 'You look amazingly sexy in that uniform,' he whispered with a wolfish grin.

'Cheeky,' she said with a laugh. 'The band was great tonight, thank you.'

'We do our best,' he said. 'Good to have Bobby and Stevie on board as well.'

'Let's grab a bite to eat then,' Fran said, taking him by the hand and leading him towards the laden table in the green room where after-show refreshments were always served to the hungry casts of shows and pantomimes. 'Hope Lorraine has been good for Mam and Dad,' she said, reaching out for a ham sandwich.

Sam nodded. 'Do you have to stay at your mam's place tonight?' he asked, raising a questioning eyebrow.

'Not really. I just go back there instead of to an empty house.'

'Well, if I come back with you it won't be empty, will it?'

'No, I don't suppose it will be,' Fran replied, trying to keep her face straight.

'Well then?'

She nodded. 'Well then.'

Early on Thursday morning and after arranging to meet up later that day, Fran and Sam said goodbye as he sneaked out to his car, which he'd parked down the bottom of the street to avoid the attention of Fran's nosy neighbour. Fran closed the door behind him and leant back against it with a contented sigh. She didn't think they'd been observed but if they had, well, she really couldn't care less. It was no one's business but hers what she, a divorced woman, did or didn't do. She brewed a pot of tea and made herself a slice of toast. She sat at the table and smiled as she thought about what a fabulous night and early morning she'd just enjoyed. The show had been one of the best she'd ever sung in and being in Sam's loving arms all night had been the icing on the cake. It felt good to be loved because Sam wanted to love her and not just because he thought she was his by rights as Frankie had done in the past. Sam had been gentle but passionate and as he'd said after the first time he'd made love to her, he didn't want to hurt her or scare her off after what she'd been through. Fran was grateful for that. She'd been nervous, but there had been no need to be.

Tonight he said he wanted to take her to the pictures if her mam would have Lorraine to stay again. Hopefully she would and then she and Sam could come back here again. She finished her breakfast and went to run herself a nice hot bath where she could relax for a while, something that was impossible when Lorraine was in the house. It was still early, so there was no rush to get to her mam's for an hour or two. She'd pop into Edie's for ten minutes when she was ready. She couldn't hear any noise coming through the walls next door yet, so Edie and Stevie must be taking advantage of Dennis being with Edie's mam and having a lie-in.

'Are you okay, Fen?' Basil asked as his wife coughed and moaned beside him. She was trying to speak but seemed to be struggling for breath. He sat up and helped her into a sitting position, placing his own pillow behind her to help prop her up. She hadn't felt too well as the show came to an end last night and he really should have insisted he bring her home, but she'd wanted to mingle with the acts in the green room, so he'd helped her into her wheelchair, which he'd put backstage while she was seated, and took her through to meet and greet everyone.

Mary had tapped his shoulder and said Fen looked pale and was coughing quite a lot and he needed to get her home to bed. He should have listened. They'd had a busy time over the last few weeks and especially Christmas week, with dinner at

Bobby and Bella's and then round to Scotty's for tea with everyone else. Maybe he should have insisted she rest more. She seemed to be exhausted now. He got out of bed and pulled on his dressing gown. It was too early to call anyone; Bobby, Bella and the kids would still be sleeping and besides, he didn't want them worrying unnecessarily. In the hall he looked for the doctor's number in Fenella's address book by the telephone and quickly dialled.

As the call was answered, Basil explained who he was and why he was ringing. The doctor told him he would be with him as soon as possible. He unlocked the front door and went to sit by the bed and held Fenella's hand. Her breathing was laboured and her skin felt clammy to the touch. Her eyes were closed but he didn't think she was sleeping. He got up and went to look out of the bedroom window, which overlooked the road they lived on. All was quiet but he spotted a familiar mop of hair on a cyclist riding down the slight incline in the road. Levi, out on his new Christmas bike that Basil and Fenella had bought for him. He banged on the window to attract his attention. Levi skidded to a halt using his best shoes as a brake. Basil winced, knowing Bella would go mad if he scraped the leather of the toes. He beckoned as Levi waved and came to the front door.

'What's up, Granddad?' Levi asked, propping his bike by the garden gate.

'Can you go home and let your mam and dad know that Granny Fen is poorly and I've sent for the doctor, please, son?'

Levi's face took on a panic-stricken look. He nodded. 'I'll send them right away and go and look after our Lizzie for them. Give Granny Fen my love.' He got back onto his bike and pedalled at speed back up the hill.

Bobby and Bella arrived soon after the doctor and Basil showed them into the lounge. 'What's wrong?' Bobby asked, looking worried.

'She can hardly breathe,' Basil told them, 'and she's gone a funny colour.'

The doctor came out of the bedroom and joined them in the lounge. 'I need to call for an ambulance,' he told them. 'She's very weak, struggling for breath. I think she has pneumonia, but we'll let a specialist confirm the diagnosis. Her body is already in a weakened state because of the multiple sclerosis. I'm afraid your wife is a very poorly lady, Mr Jenkins. I suggest you get dressed and then you can accompany her in the ambulance when it arrives.'

'Go on, Basil,' Bella encouraged. 'We'll go home and call Martin to bring us to the Royal. We'll be with you as soon as we can.'

At the hospital, Basil, Bobby and Bella sat in the small family waiting room they had been shown to while the staff made Fenella comfortable on the women's medical ward. Martin had dropped Bella and Bobby off and had gone back home so that he and Mary could see to Levi and Lizzie. He'd told them to ring the house if they needed to be picked up later. A kind nurse had brought them a tray of tea and biscuits and informed them a doctor would be with them shortly.

Bella anxiously chewed her lip and patted Bobby's hand. What an awful thing to happen so suddenly. Although when she thought back to last night, Fenella had been quieter than usual when Basil had brought her to the green room, and she had been coughing quite a lot. She glanced up at the wall clock that ticked away the minutes and sighed. She'd asked Martin to tell Mam to call the rest of their family and let them know where they were. As she mentally counted the yellow flowers on the faded patterned curtains the door flew open and Molly and Earl came into the room, both wearing anxious expressions. Bella was glad to see her sister. It was right that Earl should be here to support Basil and Bobby, and she was happy to see him too.

'Any news? 'Molly asked, sitting down beside Bella and reaching for her hand.

'Not yet,' Bella replied as a gentle tap sounded at the door and a young white-coated doctor came in.

Basil looked up as the doctor said his name. 'Mr Jenkins and Mr Harrison,' he said to Bobby and Basil, 'would you like to follow me please.'

They got to their feet, Bobby giving Bella's hand a final squeeze. She looked anxiously after them as they followed the doctor.

Molly chewed her lip, tears in her eyes. 'It's not looking good, is it? The fact they've only let two go to her, I mean.'

'Well, they are her husband and son, love,' Earl said. 'Maybe she's asked for them. Let's just wait and see before we jump to any conclusions.'

The door opened and a young cadet nurse came in, straightening her cap. 'Sally!' Molly gasped. 'Oh I'm so glad to see you, love.'

Sally smiled and swallowed hard. 'I'm just glad I'm on this ward today,' she said. 'I really love Dianna's Granny Fen. They've asked me to bring you to her bedside. She's in a private side room. If you'd like to follow me.'

Bella nodded and followed her as Sally led the way, Earl and Molly on her heels. Sally opened the door and stood back as they filed into the side room, where Fenella was tucked into a bed with an oxygen mask over her face. Chairs were arranged around the bed for them all. Basil sat at the top, holding Fenella's hand, his face pale as the noise of her laboured breathing filled the room.

'She's very poorly,' Bobby whispered to Bella as she sat beside him. 'We've been told to prepare for the worst. They've told us she has double pneumonia. It's very hard for her to take a deep breath. The MS has weakened her and her body is struggling; her lungs can't cope with much more. I don't think it's going to be long.'

Bella felt the tears running down her cheeks. Her lovely, feisty and energetic mother-in-law, always there with her support in the early days of Bella and Bobby's marriage, putting a roof over Bella's family's heads when they were desperate, helping everyone even though she'd been widowed herself, taking Levi under her wing and being a doting granny to him, and again to Dianna and Lizzie, and Molly's children, who all called her Granny Fen. A much-loved wife and business partner to Basil in later life. A true matriarch who hadn't had the easiest start in life, born into a poor family, but who had fought and worked hard to get out of the poverty trap and overcome all the odds to be the woman she became. Admired and respected by all who knew her. What on earth would they do without her? She felt Bobby's arm slip around her shoulders and was aware of Molly sobbing in Earl's arms.

Fenella slipped away at midday with her family around her. Earl and Molly had driven into the city, so they took Basil, Bobby and Bella home. Basil wanted to be alone in his own bungalow, but had promised he would call Bobby later in the day to reassure them he was okay. Earl and Molly went back to Bobby and Bella's place, where Molly set about making them all sandwiches for lunch.

As they sat on the sofas in the lounge, sipping hot sweet tea, Bobby raised his mug. 'Safe journey, Mum,' he said. 'Hope Dad's waiting to meet you at the pearly gates. Until we meet again.'

Bella sniffed. 'Bobby, that's lovely. I hope they do find one another again. I feel so sad for Basil, though. He's going to be lost and he's not in the best of health himself. We're going to have to look after him the best we can.'

'We will,' Bobby said. 'Dianna was going to be caring for Mum soon, so maybe she can look after Basil now, just be there for him as and when he needs it. I'm sure he'd like that.'

Earl and Molly nodded. 'He would, and so would Dianna.'

Fenella was laid to rest in the church graveyard next to her late husband just after New Year. The funeral was attended by all her extended family and her many WI friends, who also laid on a wake in the church hall where she had organised and helped with so many events in the past. The vicar in his eulogy spoke very highly of Fenella's kind and helpful ways towards members of the community and at the wake Basil raised a toast to his dear wife, which everyone joined in with.

Dianna sang Granny Fen's favourite hymn, 'Jerusalem', as a solo, sending a shiver down Bobby's spine. How he would miss his lovely mum; how they *all* would miss her.

'That was beautiful,' Bobby said to Bella, his voice choking on a sob. 'Mum would have been so proud to hear Di sing that.'

Bella nodded. 'She would. I think we've done her very proud all round today. She couldn't have done better if she'd organised it herself. And I bet she's here in spirit keeping an eye on us all anyway.'

Bobby smiled and raised an eyebrow before looking over his shoulder. 'It really wouldn't surprise me if you were right.'

Fran got to her feet and wiped her clammy face on a towel. She brushed her teeth and looked at her pasty appearance in the mirror. She sighed and went downstairs just as Edie let herself in at the front door, calling, 'Only me.'

'Come in,' Fran called back as she met Edie in the hallway.

'Oh God, *you* look rough!' Edie exclaimed. 'You're so pale, Fran.'

'Oh thanks. Nice to know who your friends are in times of crisis,' Fran shot back, rolling her eyes and grinning. 'Come on through, I'll put the kettle on. No doubt Bella will be here shortly also telling me I look rough.'

'No doubt.' Edie followed her into the back sitting room and took a seat at the dining table while Fran brewed a pot of tea. She carried a tray of mugs and biscuits through as Bella knocked and let herself in. 'Come on through, we're in the back,' Fran called out.

Bella came in smiling and then frowned as she caught sight of Fran's pale face. 'Oh dear, Fran. Been sick again? You look awful.'

Fran nodded. 'I'm afraid so. I'm going to see the doctor this afternoon. I can't put it off any longer. And anyway, I feel exactly the same as I did when I was first expecting Lorraine, so I'm pretty sure I must be in the family way.'

'What does Sam say about it?' Edie asked, reaching for a bourbon cream.

Fran smiled. 'He's fine. Unbelievably laid-back. We were planning on an autumn wedding anyway, as you know, so we'll just bring it forward to next month. He said as soon as we know we'll put the banns in and get organised.'

'Are you excited?' Bella asked.

'I am, very. Can't wait to be married to Sam. He's such a lovely man and with us both being in the same business he's not going to object to me getting on stage all dressed up like you-know-who did, is he?'

'Definitely not,' Bella agreed. 'And you're so right. He *is* a lovely man. I'm sure you'll be dead happy with him.'

'How far on do you think you are?' Edie asked.

'Just over eight weeks. I've missed two monthlies now.'

'Well, you're not showing yet, so you'll get away with it, I mean without any nosy neighbours giving you the knowing looks.'

Fran smiled. 'I don't care if they do. I'm past caring to be honest. I'm just too happy to be bothered by any gossips these days. I've warned me mam and she doesn't seem unduly bothered. She said I've to tell people it's arrived early if anyone says anything untoward. Anyway, never mind me, how's Basil doing?'

Bella sighed softly. 'He's a lost man, bless him. He's really gone downhill since Fen died. Doesn't shave properly and his clothes look a bit rumpled. We try and help as much as we can but he's a proud man and we don't like to interfere.'

'It's such a shame,' Edie said. 'He's a changed man all right. I wish we could do something to cheer him up but nothing seems to these days.'

'Earl said a big hit record might put a smile on his face, but we need some new songs and you're going to be busy arranging a wedding, not to mention looking after two kids soon enough,' Bella said. 'I think that will be next year's aim.'

'I can write songs too,' Fran said with a frown. 'I'll have a think later after I'm back from the doc's and I know what's what. Sam's coming for his tea tonight, so I'll have a word with him, see if we can help at all.'

'When will Sam be moving in with you?' Bella asked.

'He's giving notice on his room next week, so he'll start to move his things across then. He's not got much; it's mainly his drum kit, gramophone and records and his clothes. He rents the room furnished, so all that stuff will stay there.'

Bella looked around and frowned. 'Where are you going to put a blooming drum kit? Not to mention a new baby and all the things you'll need for it.'

Fran smiled. 'Ah well, as soon as we're married we'll get our names on the housing list. They're building that new estate in Allerton and the houses look really nice. Hopefully we might just get rehoused before the baby arrives and if not then soon after. In the meantime the drum kit will have to go in the front room.'

'Oh well, that'll be good if you can get somewhere, Allerton is not too far from us,' Bella said.

Edie frowned. 'I'll be all on me own down here then. No chance of us getting rehoused with just our Dennis, is there? They'll say we're not overcrowded.'

Fran laughed. 'Well, get cracking then. You keep saying you'd like another.'

'I would, but Stevie wants to buy us a house. He's saving for the deposit and if we have to dip into it to buy more baby stuff it will take us a lot longer. Besides, I like working at the studios and doing the odd club at the weekend, when Earl can get us bookings of course. It's just not the right time.'

'Oh, I know what I meant to tell you,' Bella began, 'but she doesn't want all of Liverpool to know so keep it to yourselves. Dianna and Stewart are getting engaged the first week of next month, the day of her twentieth birthday. How lovely is that?'

'Oh, that is wonderful,' Edie said. 'He's such a good-looking lad and Dianna is smitten with him. They make a perfect pair and he's so talented. I've seen some of his drawings and they're really very good. I'm so happy for them.'

'Me too,' Fran said, beaming. 'What does Earl say?'

'He's given them his blessing, according to our Molly. He's very happy for them. He knows Stewart will look after her and he's now working with Scotty learning the architect trade, so he's got a good future ahead of him, and if Dianna and the girls don't have a big hit record soon I'll be very surprised. I'm really glad that she chose to leave nursing. No point in her carrying on with a career that was making her unhappy. It was taking the light out of her; you could see her sparkle diminishing before your eyes. She was always so bubbly and laughing before starting that course. That blooming Sister Tutor's got a lot to answer for, treating a young girl like a skivvy. I know they all have to learn to empty a bedpan for goodness' sake, but she made sure her cousin's daughter did as little of that as possible. You only get one life and the world's changing; there are more opportunities for young girls nowadays. Singing is definitely Dianna's thing, but she had to find that out for herself and make her own choices. Earl's picked a new stage name for the girls and it seems to have gone down very well with them. He's got a song lined up that Stewart and Nigel have written and hope-fully later in the year it will go out with their new name on the label: Dianna and the Crystalettes.'

'Wow, that sounds very impressive,' Edie said.

Fran nodded her agreement. 'It's a very American name so it should suit them. They always look great together on stage, especially as their aunts make all the fabulous matching dresses they wear. They are all so alike; they look like triplets, never mind twins plus one. It's really nice to have aunts and mothers that are as talented with a needle as Dolores and Ruby are. Such a fine skill to have if *they* also ever decide to pack the nursing in.'

'I can't see them ever doing that.' Bella laughed. 'But they are indeed talented dressmakers, so you never know what the future will bring.' She drained her mug of tea and got to her feet. 'I'd better go. I need to get some shopping in. We've got Basil coming tonight for tea and I've also got my first driving lesson this afternoon.' She held her hand out and wiggled it around. 'Look at me, shaking at the thought. I am absolutely terrified. But it has to be done and it will give me so much more independence. Phone me later and let me know how you get on at the doc's, Fran. Good luck.'

Bella let herself out and strolled down Victory Street. It was a long time since she'd lived here, in her old family home next to Fran's place, but she had such happy childhood memories of the time her dad and little sister Betty were alive and they were a family of five. Such a lot of water under the bridge since those far-off days, but she'd never forget them. She was hurrying down nearby Picton Road towards the butcher's shop when she heard someone calling her name and whipped around to see her mam's best pal Ethel Hardy hurrying to catch her up. She hadn't seen Ethel since Fenella's funeral, so it was good to see her looking so well. She'd made a good recovery from her cancer a few years ago. 'Hiya, Aunty Et,' she greeted her. 'How are you doing?' She kissed her cheek as Ethel drew level with her.

'I'm good, thanks, chuck. And how are you and Bobby and the kiddies?'

'We're all fine thanks. You're looking very well.'

Ethel patted her soft curls into place. 'Apart from this grey mop you mean,' she said, laughing. 'Makes me look like an old woman. I should have a tint put on. I'm just off to get the tram over to your mam's place. She's expecting me. Martin's out all day, so we're having a catch-up and a putting the world to rights this afternoon and then going to lotto at the club tonight, or bingo or whatever they flipping call it these days.'

'Well, you have a lovely time, Aunty Et. Tell Mam I'll see her tomorrow. Hope you both get a big win tonight.'

'Thanks, chuck, me too! See you soon.' Ethel waved as she walked towards the tram stop. Bella had a sudden thought. Ethel had been on her own a long time, since her husband had been tragically killed on the railway while doing his job, many years ago. She and Basil had always got on well when they'd seen one another at the parties Fenella had thrown at her home. Maybe one night soon she should invite Ethel for tea at the same time as she invited Basil. They would be good company for one another. It was a little too soon to be playing Cupid for Basil, but the pair were already good friends and Basil certainly needed to get out and socialise a bit more. Since Fenella died he barely spoke to anyone outside of his nearest family and Earl. His next-door neighbours had tried to include him in various activities and had invited him to join their crown green bowling team but he'd politely declined their offer. He'd told Bella and Bobby that it was mainly old people on the team and he wasn't quite ready for that sort of lifestyle yet. She'd ask Mam tomorrow what she thought of the idea. A little smile playing on her face, Bella hurried into the butcher's and joined the queue.

Fran hurried back from the doctor's, a big smile on her face and excited butterflies dancing around in her stomach. Her new baby was due sometime in the New Year and when she'd seen a

midwife at the clinic next week she would have a definite date.
The doctor was sending off a urine sample to confirm, but he'd
examined her, and with the information she'd given him he'd
said that he was in no doubt. She couldn't wait to tell Sam. Edie
would let her use her phone to call him, so she made her way
back to Victory Street, stopping on the way to buy a couple of
vanilla slices at the bakery. This news was worthy of more than
biscuits, she thought. Pity Bella would now have gone home,
but she could phone her after talking to Sam at his lodgings.

Edie let her in the front door and Fran knew that the look
on her face would say it all and she wouldn't need to ask. 'Can I
use the phone to call Sam please?' she asked.

'Be my guest,' Edie said, taking the white paper bag from
Fran's trembling hands. 'Congratulations and you'd better call
Bella as soon as you've finished with Sam. I'll go and get the tea
brewed. I'm so happy for you, Fran,' she finished, a big smile on
her face.

Fran dialled Sam's lodgings' communal number and it was
answered immediately. He'd known she had a doctor's appointment this afternoon, so would have been anxiously awaiting her
call.

'It's a yes,' she told him, holding her breath just in case he
told her to get lost and he didn't want anything more to do with
her. But his yell of excitement told her she was being stupid to
even think along those lines. She finished her call in tears and
dialled Bella's number. Bella burst into tears too and congratulated her and said she would catch up tomorrow. Fran went to
join Edie, who had steaming mugs of tea waiting and the vanilla
slices out on plates.

'So what did he say?' Edie asked, pushing the sugar bowl
across to Fran, who had flopped down on a chair and was
fanning her face with her hand.

'He's thrilled to bits. He's picking me up in an hour and
then we are going to Wavertree Town Hall to book a wedding

for next month. Phew.' Fran took a sip of tea and smiled. 'I need to go and root out my birth certificate and my decree absolute. They're in a box in the wardrobe, so that won't take me long. Then I'll nip round to me mam's and tell her. She can tell Dad and me brothers. I doubt they'll be that upset, they just want me to be happy. The new niece or nephew will be a bonus. And you and Bella can come shopping with me on Saturday to choose an outfit.'

~

As Bella put the phone down she did a little jig of happiness for her friend. Sam was a lovely man and she knew that Fran and Lorraine would be well looked after by him. Her mind went quickly into overdrive. That would be two celebration parties coming up: Fran's wedding day and Dianna's engagement. Both Basil and Aunty Et would be invited. It was an ideal opportunity to seat the pair close to one another. She called her mam and told her of Fran's news and also asked her if she thought it might be a good idea to encourage a closer friendship between Ethel and Basil. Her mam was quiet for a moment while she mulled over the idea.

Finally she spoke. 'I don't see why not, chuck. They get on well. They'd be company for one another. I know both of them get quite lonely, rattling around in houses on their own. I tell you what, at the weekend me and Martin will have them both over for Sunday dinner. Let's see how that goes. Leave it with me. I know you've got Basil coming tonight for his tea. I'll ring him while he's there at yours. He doesn't always answer his phone at home and that worries me.'

'Good idea, Mam. I'll answer and then get him to come to the phone. Talk to you later then.'

'You will, chuck, and congratulate Fran from me and Martin. I'm glad she's found happiness with Sam.'

. . .

'What about this one?' Bella held up a smart linen fabric two-piece suit in a soft apple-green shade. 'It's lovely and light for a summer wedding and the green suits your colouring, Fran. And it's something you can wear again as well.' The girls were in Lewis's department store picking out an outfit for Fran's wedding day, as well as choosing new dresses for themselves that they could double up for the wedding and Dianna's engagement party.

'You could have cream and orange roses in your bouquet,' Edie suggested. 'And if you fastened your hair into a French pleat you could have little cream silk roses threaded through. You'd look lovely.'

Fran chewed her lip and nodded slowly. 'Do you think so? It *is* nice and like you say, I can wear it again.'

'Go and try it on,' Bella said. 'While we have a root through that rail of dresses over there. Give us a shout when you're ready.'

Fran took the green suit to the fitting rooms and an assistant took charge. Bella could hear her gushing over how the colour would suit her lovely red hair. She grinned. Fran would go mad. Her hair was a rich deep shade of auburn and she hated people saying she was a redhead. Her attention was caught by Edie holding up a lovely pale blue full-skirted dress with her favoured sweetheart neckline and button-front bodice.

'What do you think?' Edie asked. 'I've already got some new white peep-toe sandals and a matching bag as well.'

Bella nodded. 'Just the job. No point in spending the money when you've already got things to wear.'

'I'll go and try it on then,' Edie said. 'Have a look and see what you can find for yourself.'

Bella's keen eye had already spotted a flash of rich cerise pink on the rail. As Edie strolled towards the fitting rooms she pulled a stunning silk dress from among the other garments hanging there. It was a shirtwaister style with buttons all the way down the front, a small turn-back collar and elbow-length sleeves with matching cuffs. The buttons were clear glass and twinkled as light caught them. A sash of the same fabric formed a belt around the middle. Immediately, Bella thought of her navy high-heeled shoes that would contrast perfectly. All she would need was a small matching bag. And the dress would be lovely for the engagement party Earl and Molly were planning to throw for Dianna and Stewart. Bobby had told her to buy whatever took her fancy. She'd need to kit Levi and Lizzie out as well, but that could be done next weekend. She made her way to the fitting rooms just as Edie and Fran appeared to show off the new clothes. 'Oh you both look wonderful,' Bella said, clapping her hand to her mouth and feeling emotional. This was bringing back memories of the last time they'd chosen wedding outfits for their Bryant Sisters triple wedding at the end of the war. Then they'd all worn identical full-length ivory lace dresses. 'The green suits you so well, Fran, and that blue is perfect on you, Edie.'

Edie beamed. 'Great! That's me sorted then.'

'And me,' Fran said. 'What have you got there? I love that colour. You always did suit rich pinks when we were on stage with ENSA. With you being dark-haired and brown-eyed you can carry it off so well.'

'Thanks,' Bella said. 'I'll just try it on for size and if it fits that's us three done and dusted. We can go to the Kardomah for a coffee and cake before going home. Might as well make the most of a morning of freedom.' Bella hurried into the fitting room and Fran and Edie got changed back into their own clothes while she tried on the dress. She gazed at her reflection and turned this way and that, lifting her long hair upwards. Satisfied it looked just fine, she stepped out of the curtained cubicle.

'Wow! That looks gorgeous on you,' Fran said as Edie nodded her approval. 'Well, that's us three sorted. Who was it that said women take all day to choose an outfit? They know nothing. Do we need hats? You know I hate wearing them.'

'So do I,' Bella agreed. 'Just do as Edie suggested then and thread little silk rosebuds in your hair, Fran. I might do the same. Right, I'll just get changed and then we'll go and get that coffee we promised ourselves.'

Dianna gazed at the sparkling diamond solitaire on the third finger of her left hand and smiled. Everyone cheered and shouted their congratulations as Stewart drew her into his arms and planted a kiss on her lips. Earl stood proudly by Molly's side and cheered loudest of all. They were all outside in the back garden and the day was warm and dry. Molly had decorated the trees and bushes with bunting she had saved from the war and it brightened everywhere up. She had laid a buffet tea out on a couple of trestle tables that were also decorated with bunting fastened onto white cloths and looked lovely. Basil opened champagne and poured glasses for the adults while Mary poured lemonade for the children. He tapped a spoon against his glass to gain attention, then toasted the young couple's future happiness.

'Wishing every happiness to Dianna and Stewart. Many congratulations.' Everyone raised their glasses in a toast.

'Thank you,' Stewart said. 'And thank you to Molly and Earl for holding this lovely party for us. I'm so looking forward to being a part of this extended family and so are my parents.' He nodded in the direction of a middle-aged, smartly dressed couple who were beaming with happiness, and both raised their glasses towards him and Dianna. His dad smiled and stepped forward.

'I can't tell you how proud your mother and I are to have this beautiful young woman as our future daughter-in-law,' he said as everyone cheered again. He looked towards Earl. 'Well done, sir, for raising such a charming and talented young lady.'

'Well thank you kindly,' Earl said. 'Molly here and my good sister Ruby had a hand in her upbringing as well. She's certainly a daughter to be very proud of.'

'Dad,' Dianna said, rolling her eyes. 'Stop it now, you're embarrassing me.'

'I'm only speaking the truth, princess,' Earl said. 'Isn't that right?' he said to Ruby and Molly, who were standing nearby.

Aunt Ruby nodded. 'He sure is. We are all very proud of her.'

'All we need now is a number one hit record,' Basil chipped in and everyone laughed and nodded their agreement. 'All in good time,' he continued. 'I feel it in my water that it will happen next year. We need to compete with America and all this new rock and roll stuff they're writing and recording.' He took a seat in a deckchair alongside Bella. 'Ah that's better,' he said, sighing with relief. 'Take the weight off my poor aching legs. There's no fun in this getting old lark, Bella.'

Bella smiled. 'I'm sure there isn't,' she said, spotting Aunty Ethel standing beside her mam. 'Aunty Et, do you want a seat while I go and see what our Lizzie's up to,' she called. Ethel's face lit up and she strolled across the garden as Bella got up from the chair.

'Thanks, queen. My legs were just about to pack in.'

'Oh, same as mine,' Basil said, taking Ethel's glass from her hand while she flopped down and got herself comfortable. He handed it back and clinked his glass against hers. 'Cheers, my dear.'

'And cheers to you too, Basil,' Ethel said, smiling.

Bella strode across the lawn towards her mam, grinning, leaving the pair comparing their aches and pains. 'It's a start,' she whispered as she drew close to Mary.

'It all helps,' Mary said. 'And the last two Sundays when they've come for dinner they've got on like a house on fire as always, so here's hoping. They have a lovely friendship already, which is always a good start.'

'Dad, can we play some music on your radiogram?' Levi asked. 'We can sing along then.'

'Go on then, son. Be very careful though. Don't you scratch any of my records.'

Levi rolled his eyes and disappeared inside as the garden gate creaked open and Sally and Nigel strolled up the path.

Dianna squealed and rushed over to her friend. 'Oh I'm so glad you could make it. I wasn't sure what shift you were on. Stewart told me Nige said you were going to try and get here. It's good to see you both.'

'Congratulations,' Sally said, giving them both hugs. 'So very happy for you both.'

'Me too,' Nigel said. 'Wish we could get engaged but Sally's not allowed while she's training.'

'Can't you do it secretly?' Stewart asked.

'Secretly?' Sally raised her eyebrows and laughed. 'Not a chance of having a secret from anyone in that blooming nurses' home. Carol and all the girls send you their love, Di. They're all working today but said if you give plenty of notice when you get married they'll book time off in advance.'

Dianna smiled. 'We will do. But it will be a few years until we can afford it.' She wasn't sure when they would be able to get married or afford a house, but for the first time she wasn't in a hurry to plan out her entire life. She was happy to be there with Stewart, surrounded by friends and family, and just enjoy the moment.

Upstairs in the bedroom, Bella and Edie were finished fixing the cream rosebuds in Fran's French pleat when they heard the clatter of the letter box. Sam had been shipped off to his mate's house last night as Fran had told him it was bad luck to see the bride before the ceremony, even when you lived with her. She didn't want to risk the day being jinxed in any way. Bella ran downstairs to pick up the post, which appeared to be a couple of cards and a letter from America in a pale blue envelope.

Fran and Edie made their way downstairs and Bella handed the post to Fran. They sat down to wait for Basil, who was picking them up to take them to the register office. Fran opened the cards and announced that one was from her aunt and uncle in Southport and the other from Frankie's sister, who had kept in touch, wishing them well. 'That's nice of her,' Fran said. 'Sheila has always been on my side. They all disowned him but Sheila wanted to keep in touch with me so she could see how her niece was doing.' She opened the blue envelope and smiled. 'Ah that's nice. It's from the Jessops in America. What good timing with the post as she's wishing us all the best. She says your mam told her I'm getting married, Bella.'

Bella nodded. 'Yes, Mam said she'd told them last time she wrote to them. How lovely that they wrote to you.'

A knock sounded at the front door and Bella hurried to answer it. It was Basil, looking very smart in a new navy suit and tie with a crisp white shirt and a white carnation in his buttonhole. Bella observed how much better he was looking lately. Back to his neat and tidy self. He was missing Fenella, there was no doubt about that, but he seemed to be picking himself up a bit since he'd got friendlier with Aunty Ethel. *Long may it continue*, Bella thought. 'We're ready, Basil, come on inside for a minute. The net curtains are twitching across the street!'

Basil laughed and followed Bella down the narrow hall into the back sitting room where Edie was sorting out Fran's bouquet of orange and cream roses. 'Well, what can I say,' he said, his eyes filling with a sudden rush of tears. 'My beautiful girls all back together and looking a million dollars. Just like you all did when I first found you and signed you up for ENSA. So many things have happened since that night, both good and not so good, but you three will always do me proud. You're the daughters I never had and I love you all dearly. Come on, girls; let's get you on the way to a very happy future, one that will hopefully make all our dreams come true.'

A LETTER FROM PAM

Dear reader,

I want to say a huge thank you for choosing to read *The Daughters of Victory Street*. If you did enjoy it, and want to keep up to date with all my latest releases, just sign up at the following link. Your email address will never be shared and you can unsubscribe at any time.

www.bookouture.com/pam-howes

To my loyal band of regular readers who bought and reviewed my previous Bryant Sisters stories, thank you for waiting patiently for this fourth book. Your support is most welcome and very much appreciated.

As always a big thank you to Beverley Ann Hopper and Sandra Blower and the members of their FB group Book Lovers. Thanks for all the support you show me. Also thank you to Deryl Easton and the supportive members of her FB group Gangland Governors/NotRights. Thank you to Claire Lyons and her beautiful son Riley who is my inspiration for Bella and Earl's son, Levi. As always, Claire's daily FB updates of Riley are a joy.

A huge thank you to team Bookouture, especially my lovely editor Sonny, it's been a pleasure to work with you again, and also thanks to Jacqui, Lauren and Becca.

And last but definitely not least, thank you to our amazing

media team, Kim Nash, Sarah Hardy and Noelle Holton for everything you do for us. You're "Simply the Best" as Tina would say! And thanks also to the gang in the Bookouture Authors' Lounge for always being there. As always, I'm so proud to be one of you.

I hope you loved *The Daughters of Victory Street* and if you did I would be very grateful if you could write a review. I'd love to hear what you think, and it makes such a difference helping new readers to discover one of my books for the first time.

I love hearing from my readers – you can get in touch on my Facebook page, through Twitter, Goodreads or my website.

Thanks,

Pam Howes

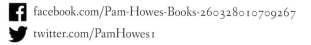

facebook.com/Pam-Howes-Books-260328010709267

twitter.com/PamHowes1

ACKNOWLEDGEMENTS

For my lovely and supportive partner, my gorgeous girls, my assorted grandchildren, and my new great granddaughter; their wives, husbands and partners, and the rest of my family, as always. Thanks for all your support and love over the last couple of horrible years of loss and sadness. Thanks also to my dear friends Brenda Thomasson and Sue Hulme for beta reading. Much appreciated as always. Lots of love to you all. Xxx

Printed in Great Britain
by Amazon